M. L. BURTON

crimilia

Crimilia

Meredith Leigh Burton

Tate Publishing & *Enterprises*

This novel is a work of fiction. Names, descriptions, entities, and incidents included in the story are products of the author's imagination. Any resemblance to actual persons, events, and entities is entirely coincidental.

The opinions expressed by the author are not necessarily those of Tate Publishing, LLC.

Published by Tate Publishing & Enterprises, LLC
127 E. Trade Center Terrace | Mustang, Oklahoma 73064 USA
1.888.361.9473 | www.tatepublishing.com

Tate Publishing is committed to excellence in the publishing industry. The company reflects the philosophy established by the founders, based on Psalm 68:11,
"The Lord gave the word and great was the company of those who published it."

Cover design by Blake Brasor
Interior design by Joel Uber

Published in the United States of America

ISBN: 978-1-61739-981-7
1. Fiction; Christian, Classic & Allegory
2. Fiction; Christian, Fantasy
11.01.31

dedication

In thanksgiving and appreciation to Jesus Christ, my Lord, who is the true "Freedom's Bread," (John 6-35). He is the One who makes me see.

Also to my niece, Tristyn Layla Burton. I pray she'll grow to love reading as much as I do.

acknowledgments

I'd like to thank God the Father and the Holy Spirit for planting this idea and for giving me so many gifts.

I'd also like to thank my marvelous family. They've done more for me than they will ever know. God bless you all. A special thanks is due to my mother, Carol Burton, proofreader extraordinaire, to Jessica Robinson, whose kind words about the rough draft meant so much, and to my aunt, Brenda Pollock, a true computer genius!

Thanks also to Dr. Mila Truan, the woman who introduced me to the joys of reading; unlocking multiple doors for me. Her encouragement and love have helped me through so many trials. My appreciation can never fully be expressed!

Laura stared but did not stir,
Longed but had no money;
The whisk-tailed merchant bade her taste
In tones as smooth as honey...
She sucked and sucked and sucked the more
Fruits which that unknown orchard bore…

—Christina Rossetti, “Goblin Market.”

Table of Contents

bitterness and bus rides

"Hannah! Breakfast!" The shrill screech of Ms. Maplewood's voice pierced Hannah Wilkins' eardrums. Sighing, she flopped onto her stomach, the bedsprings creaking under her weight. She burrowed farther down into the warm cocoon of sheets.

"Hannah! Did you hear me, young lady?" Ms. Maplewood's shrill voice rose two more octaves. "The school bus'll be here in ten minutes!"

Hannah jerked the bedclothes away. Her bare feet hit the carpeted floor with a muffled thud.

"I'm coming!" she screamed.

Going to her dresser, she groped in the top drawer for a pair of socks. She selected a pair and felt inside them. When her fingers encountered the bundles of stitches sewn into the socks, she began counting. Three sets of stitches.

Red, she thought. *Perfect.* Red was her favorite color.

After Hannah had finished dressing, she went to the corner beside the door. Taking a slender, long white object from its place, she trudged down the stairs.

"Well, you took your time!" Ms. Maplewood fumed. "Your oatmeal's getting cold!"

"Yuck! Why are we always having oatmeal?"

"Because we are! Now eat up."

Hannah jabbed her spoon into the thickening mess. Slowly, she stirred the gloppy concoction round and round the bowl. She smelled coffee and heard the trickle of liquid being poured into Ms. Maplewood's cup.

"Your mom's working late tonight. What would you like for supper?"

Hannah thrust a spoonful of oatmeal into her mouth. She chewed and grimaced in disgust. Mom was working late.

So what else is new? she thought savagely.

"Spaghetti's fine," she mumbled.

"We had that last night."

"Well, we had oatmeal yesterday!" Hannah shot back.

Ms. Maplewood sighed. "I'm really trying, you know," she said. "You could meet me halfway."

Hannah glared. She drank her milk and pushed the oatmeal bowl away.

From outside, a horn blasted. Hannah rose and took the long white object from the corner. Swinging it at an arc in front of her, she trudged toward the door.

"Have a good day," Ms. Maplewood called, "and remember your eye appointment after school. I'll meet you when the bell rings."

Hannah didn't bother to reply. Why go to the appointment? What was the use? Doctor Franklin's voice erupted in her mind. "We'll do what we can, but the optic nerves have undergone massive trauma. I must tell you that recovery is not promising." After two unsuccessful operations, Hannah no longer held out any hope. She trudged out the door and walked toward the roaring motor of the school bus.

"Hey there, Han!" Mr. Peterson called jovially. His deep, rich voice echoed over the roaring motor. "Your seat's empty today."

"Thanks," Hannah said. She lumbered up the bus steps, the object in her hand touching each step as she climbed.

"That cane comes in handy, huh?" Mr. Peterson asked.

"It's all right," Hannah admitted. Until she'd received the cane in the mail two weeks ago, she'd had to rely on the guidance of others. She still shuddered at the embarrassing thought.

Hannah settled herself into the seat directly facing Mr. Peterson. She would have preferred a back seat, but by law she was required to sit at the front.

As the bus pulled away from the house, Hannah heard the chatter of students. Of course, none of the talking concerned her. The students hadn't included her in their conversations ever since the accident

After fifteen minutes, the bus lurched as it turned into a gravel driveway. The brakes screeched as Mr. Peterson pulled to a stop.

Hannah heard the *clomp-swoosh* sound of a leg brace scraping along the gravel.

Oh, no! she thought in panic. *Not Brandon*!

But already Mr. Peterson's voice was ringing out. "Hey there, Brand! Long time no see! You feelin' better? Your mom doin' all right?"

"Sure, Mr. P! Where should I sit?"

"Your seat's still got a free spot. Come on up."

Hannah heard Brandon Pringle's leg brace clomping on the steps and knew it would take him a few minutes to get on board. She thought of making her way to a seat farther back, but she knew Brandon had probably already seen her. He had always been nice to her, but he was one of the popular kids. It wasn't fair! Why hadn't the accident made him as angry as it had made her?

Brandon finally made it onto the bus. He plopped down in the seat beside Hannah.

"Hey there, Hannah! What's shakin'?"

"Nothing," she snapped.

"You gotta cane, huh? Can you use it for a weapon too? It'd be good for self-defense."

"Knock it off!"

"Hey, lighten up. I know what you're goin' through. You ever think of that? I can't play baseball anymore. You still have your music."

"Yeah, right. Like you know."

Brandon sighed. "How's things in Mr. Muhler's class?"

"Fine. We finished *Hatchet*. Now we're reading *Roll of Thunder, Hear My Cry*."

"I've read them. *Hatchet* was the bomb!"

"I like *Roll of Thunder* the best. T.J.'s my favorite."

"Yeah, he thinks he's so cute, though."

Hannah nodded. How could she explain that the character T.J. didn't know where he belonged, like her?

"Hey, Brand! You through talkin' to Fatso yet?" The voice was nasally and male. Hannah caught a whiff of Wrigley's spearmint gum. Gross. Gordon Hamilton! He was Brandon's friend, and he always sat two seats from the front with Georgia Stafford. Hannah heard Georgia's snicker over the motor.

Brandon fidgeted nervously. "How're you, Gordon?"

"Fine. I feel sorry for you havin' to sit with her, though!"

At that moment, Hannah heard a piercing screech followed by an earsplitting boom.

"It's a deer!" Mr. Peterson shouted. The bus rocked crazily. The smell of rubber and smoke made her cough. Kids screamed. Hannah felt a strong hand grip her arm. Then she felt a tremendous jarring sensation. In an instant, she was lifted from her seat as the bus shook and shuddered. Her head cracked against the window, and she knew no more.

how did he know?

Brandon's head spun crazily. His mind churned with confusion.

Gradually, he became aware of dazzling sunlight. He felt grass beneath his feet and heard voices and the musical cadence of rushing water. What in the world?

As Brandon's eyes slowly adjusted to the blinding sunlight, he realized that he was standing on a riverbank. Scraggly trees and bushes could be seen. He also saw sparse quantities of grass and small clumps of vegetation.

"Turn from the fold of Salak, the False Reflector!" a resonant voice boomed.

Brandon jumped. He spotted a burly young man standing at the edge of the river. The man wore a camel-hair suit.

Brandon watched as the man stared after a group of departing people. There were about ten people in the group. Brandon noticed that most of the people wore looks of contempt. However, about four of them wore smiles as if heavy loads had been lifted from their shoulders. *Okay, Brandon! Get a grip! This is insane.*

The man reached into a cloth pouch attached to a leather belt around his waist. He withdrew a leathery-looking object and prepared to pop it into his mouth.

Brandon hobbled forward. Piercing pain shot up his bad leg, but he ignored it. He thought he'd seen—No, it couldn't be! Surely the man wasn't going to eat a—

The man placed the object into his mouth and chewed with relish. Brandon's stomach somersaulted. He did eat it! I don't believe this!

"Ugh! That's disgusting! You just ate a grasshopper!"

The burly man spun around. He peered closely into Brandon's dazed eyes and blinked in surprise.

"That's right, young man!" his voice boomed. "You want one? I've just procured a batch of the best wild honey around! Nothing like it for improving the taste!"

"You're nuts!"

The man surveyed the speaker closely. "You're certainly strange, my friend. What a peculiar object you have on your leg. Are you quite well?"

"Yeah, I'm just, um—I was in a car accident two years ago. I just had another operation, but I still have to wear the brace."

"Car accident? Brace? I do not understand."

Brandon shrugged. "I, um, I don't understand either. Where am I?"

"Where are you? You're at the River Pridar."

"The what?"

"The River Pridar. In Crimilia."

"Crimilia? You are nuts! I'm out of here."

Brandon turned to walk away. Then he turned back. "Have you seen a girl around here? She's kinda heavy-set, and she's carrying a cane."

The man's face was a mask of total bewilderment. "I don't know what you're referring to, but I think you'd better stay with me for the time being. My name's Jordan Ernest. If I can't interest you in my food, could I get you some willow tea? Best thing in the world for building strength!"

"Sure. Thanks." Jordan took a clay pot from the ground and filled it with water. "If you'll gather some sticks, we'll see about fixing that tea."

Brandon decided he'd better play along. He turned and began to scan the ground.

Suddenly, he heard approaching footsteps. He straightened and saw Jordan rushing forward. His face was aglow with excitement. "It's you!" he cried jovially. "The Imperial One!"

"And your cousin too, remember?" A young man approached. He was dressed in a simple robe of home-spun brown cloth. His hands bore numerous calluses, and his every movement seemed to convey a purpose. He was not handsome, but Brandon was awed by his authoritative air. The man's voice was not a cultured one. His accent, like the other man's, reminded Brandon of those British shows his mom liked to watch Sundays on public television. Wasn't that accent called

Cockney? However, his voice was gentle and loud enough that there was no possibility of misunderstanding his words. "It's great to see you, Jordan! You still eating those grasshoppers?"

Jordan laughed. "They're good! Besides, they're the easiest things to find out here. How's Aunt Marigold?"

"She's well. Marshall's with her now."

"Is he speaking to you yet?"

A cloud passed over the young man's face. "No, but he's with Mother. That's the important thing."

"But he's your brother! If you can't depend on family, then—"

"Even if my family disowns me, I have a job to do."

"Of course you do! I'm glad you came to see me first."

"I need you to do something for me."

Jordan's mouth flew open in surprise. "You mean—"

"Yes."

"But you should be the one who—"

"No. It is important that I obey my Father in all things."

Jordan nodded in understanding. "Come."

He led the man to the River Pridar. Stooping down, he reached into the mud on the riverbank, withdrawing a plain, oval-shaped mirror carved from walnut wood. "Do you pledge to turn away from Salak's rule?"

The young man nodded. Jordan held the mud-caked mirror before the man's face. "Look into the Mirror of Cleansing and follow me," he instructed.

The man stared into the mirror. Jordan waded into the waist-deep water, and the man followed. Jordan took hold of the man's shoulders. He was about to plunge the man underneath the flowing water when Jordan gasped. "The mirror!"

His eyes straining with curiosity, Brandon inched close enough to look. The glass, once mud-caked and grimy, was sparkling clean! It shown with a dazzling brilliance that was blinding!

Smiling, the young man murmured, "Proceed, Jordan."

Jordan swallowed in amazement. "In the Imperial Lord's name, I now purify you." Gently, he lowered the man's head under the water. The mirror also was dunked into the crystal pool.

When the young man rose from the water, his hair dripping, his face was aglow with purpose and wonder.

"Thank you, my cousin and friend."

Instantly, a dazzling light pierced the sun-filled sky overhead. Brandon covered his eyes. A rumbling voice reverberated around them. "My son! Well done! I am exceedingly proud!"

"Oh, Jamal! You are ready for your mission!" Jordan cried in ecstasy. He patted Jamal on the shoulder. "I still hope you'll come around."

Jamal laughed. "Sure, but why not go back to Nunmal? Aunt Eliza's really been missing you."

"I'll go back soon, but—"

Suddenly, Jordan turned to Brandon. "I'm sorry, lad! Where are my manners? This is the Imperial One!"

Brandon was dumbfounded. "What're you talking about?"

"This is my cousin, Jamal. Go with him."

Jamal turned his shining face on Brandon. "Hello, my friend. You're a long way from home!" His eyes twinkled.

"Um, yeah, you could say that! Look, straighten this guy out, will you? He says we're somewhere called Crimilia. I'm looking for a girl. The bus—"

"No need to explain, Brandon." The voice was gentle. "I cannot stay here long. I must go to Salak's palace."

"What!" Jordan roared. "You're going to that—"

"I'm going to see Lucinda. I must."

"But she'll—"

"I know."

"Look! You guys are insane!" Brandon's patience had reached a breaking point. "I need some answers here, and I need them now!"

Jamal smiled. "Stay here with Jordan, and he'll explain everything to you. If you desire to come with me later, I'll come back by to collect you. Right now, I must go. You cannot come to the palace yet. You'd be in danger." Without another word, Jamal threw his arms around his cousin's neck. Then he hurried away.

"Well, Brandon is it? How about that tea now?"

Brandon began searching along the ground for some sticks.

This has to be a dream, he thought.

It wasn't until he'd collected enough wood to build a fire that a thought slapped him upside his head. "Jordan, how'd that man know my name?"

the mirror of revelation

The room was dark and cool. On the walls, jeweled tapestries shone with many colors: crimson, topaz, aquamarine, and peach.

In the center of the room on a golden throne, a slender woman sat ensconced among plush cushions. Her heart-shaped face was framed by billowing strawberry blonde locks. Ice blue eyes shone from the alabaster pallor of her skin. Her face was devoid of expression, and it rarely ever registered emotion of any kind.

The woman wore a crimson dress of the finest silk covered in every imaginable jewel: ruby, emerald, jasper, diamond, and dozens of other precious stones.

On a table before her sat the remains of a lavish meal: a rare T-bone steak, crabmeat, a dish of creamed cauliflower, and a slab of chocolate cake.

The woman held up a commanding hand, and a man in the corner looked up inquiringly. "Bring me my mirror!"

The man nodded and withdrew. The woman leaned back with a satisfied sigh.

In a moment, he returned. "Here is your mirror, my queen."

"You may leave now."

The man placed a large cherry-framed mirror on a pearl-encrusted stand before his mistress. Then he left.

The queen leant forward. The mirror was made of imported Venetian glass studded with strange, unnamed gems of indescribable beauty. Only the queen knew that the stones were the Gems of Discord, deadly objects that lay entombed in the bowels of Crimilia's wastelands. The Queen had dispatched many servants to collect these gems, and many had not survived the task. However, she did procure enough Discord Gems to fashion her greatest tool: the Mirror of Revelation. This mirror served as her looking glass and spying tool. With it, she could closely monitor all of her subjects and summon them when necessary.

On the cherry-colored frame of this mirror, small pictures of flowers and blooming trees swayed in a lifelike breeze. In the center of the frame, the picture that held a prominent place was a carving of a rose. The rose dwarfed all the other carvings. Its petals opened wide as if spreading its perfume throughout the room. Only if you looked closely could you distinguish the small carving out of cherry wood that emerged from the center of the rose. The carving was of a scarlet serpent coiled as if to strike.

Running a crimson-nailed hand through her hair, the queen peered into the glass. She stared in rapture at her breathtaking image.

Suddenly, the throne room door crashed open. "Queen Salak! The guards have found a girl wandering about the palace grounds!" a black-cloaked man yelled.

Salak looked up from her perusal. She fixed a steely gaze upon the man. "Aufeld. What is that to me? Do what you like with her."

"Your Majesty, you might want to see this girl! She wears strange garments and carries a peculiar object."

"Ah, a foreigner, eh? As I said, she's no concern of mine."

"She's blind, my queen!" Aufeld cried desperately.

Salak sucked in her breath. Her left hand convulsed as it slapped the arm of her throne. "It can't be!"

"I thought it best to come to you right away."

Salak bit her lip so hard flecks of blood appeared on the marble-sculpted skin. "Bring her to me," she whispered in icy tones.

When the throne room door closed, Salak rose. She began to pace like an enraged lion. "You're wasting your time!" she shouted into thin air.

She returned to her mirror and gazed fixedly into its depths. Her own face showed crystal clear. A twisted smile suffused her pale features.

I'll win the game, notwithstanding, she thought darkly.

Then Salak rotated her mirror. "Show me Jamal," she murmured.

The glass clouded, and she peered transfixed at the image of her enemy. He was moving determinedly forward, purpose driven, and refusing to look back.

Yes, she thought, *keep coming closer, my friend. I'm waiting!*

The throne room door opened, and Aufeld propelled a young girl forward. The girl was struggling in his iron grip. "Let me go!" she screeched. The girl wore a red, short-sleeved shirt and blue pants woven from a coarse-looking material. "Let me go, or I'll call the police!"

"Stop squirming, you little wench!" Aufeld roared.

"Aufeld," Salak's voice crooned gently, "there's no need to alarm our guest. Release her."

"But, Your Highness—"

"Do as I say," Salak whispered.

Growling deep in his throat, the man complied. He thrust Hannah toward the throne after roughly throwing the cane at her. The cane clattered to the floor. Hannah stumbled.

"Where am I? Somebody help me!" Hannah shouted. She feverishly groped for her cane.

A hand brushed hers as the cane was handed back. "Is this what you're looking for, my dear?" Salak's voice was gentle and bell-like. Soft and refined, it held a tone of authority.

"Thank you," Hannah managed to whisper. "Where am I?"

"You're in Plenty Palace in the Land of Crimilia. Are you from Normdal or Luciana, our neighboring countries? What is your name?"

"I'm Hannah Wilkins. I'm from Tennessee."

"Tennessee? What land is that?" the woman asked sharply.

"It's in the United States. This must be England. Your accent—"

"England? You are a strange child. How did you acquire that large swelling on your head?"

"I don't know!" Hannah cried in frustration.

"Aufeld! Have Louise doctor that bump on her head, and get some food inside her. Then bring her back to me."

Aufeld nodded. "Come, child," he said gruffly.

"You're not grabbing me this time!" Hannah snapped.

Salak laughed a bubbling laugh. "Of course not, my dear! You may use the peculiar apparatus you brought with you."

"It's called a cane," Hannah informed her. Then she turned to follow her guide.

When the throne room door had closed, the queen turned back to her mirror. "Reveal to me all the information about Hannah Wilkins," she instructed. The mirror shimmered, and Salak leaned forward to peer at images of the girl's life. She smiled in satisfaction. Everything would work out to her advantage.

the mark of allegiance

"Now, are you refreshed, Brandon?" Jordan called.

"Yes, sir. Thanks," Brandon admitted. "I hate to say it, but those grasshoppers weren't bad."

Jordan laughed. "What'd I tell you? Now, you might want to prepare yourself. We have a busy afternoon ahead of us."

"Why? What's going on?"

"Ah! Many people will come! They always do. They want to be free."

"Free from what?"

"Free from their own bitterness and pride. Free from that tyrannical, harpy Salak, formerly known as Lucinda!" Jordan's voice was bitter.

"I realize that this Queen Salak or Lucinda must be mean, but I still don't understand what she's done. Why does she have two names?"

"Ah! Now that is a long story! Look around you and tell me what you see."

Bewildered, Brandon obeyed. "I see scraggly trees and grass. Why?"

"Look more closely and listen."

As Brandon looked, he saw that though the vegetation was sparse, it was multi-colored and beautiful. Jasmine-colored bushes, apricot-colored trees, and the emerald green grass took his breath away. He also listened and became entranced by the music of the river. He briefly thought about the art supplies he'd bought last year with his birthday money. Brandon couldn't explain why, but since the accident he'd become more aware of his surroundings. He thought about the beautiful colors of the landscape and longed to capture them on canvas. Of course, he'd never admit this desire to anyone. Certain things were expected of athletes even if they no longer played sports. "Everything's beautiful," he whispered.

"Yes. Salak was once as beautiful as these so-called scraggly plants. Her name was Lucinda, which means Light-Giver or Brilliant One. If you ever meet her, you'll discover that she is beautiful outwardly, but inwardly she is a dark chasm. She was an Eaglia or message bearer who once served the Imperial Lord, but her jealousy drove her away from his presence. She seduced our great mother and father and forced them from the Imperial Lord's paradise. Her name was changed to Salak, which means deformer and poisoner. Now, she turns sister against sister."

"Isn't that supposed to be brother against brother?"

"Not with the first family. Look, let me show you."

So saying, Jordan removed a small, cloth-covered book from the inside of a hollow tree. He handed it to Brandon. "Our first mother's journal," he explained.

Seething with curiosity, Brandon opened the book and blinked in surprise. "There's nothing written here!"

Jordan snorted. "Of course not!" He flipped three pages forward in the small book, touched a finger to the center of the page, and whispered: "Mother Evelina, reveal the story of Camilla and Abigail." Turning to Brandon, he continued. "She preserved her memories in this book in order to tell the story of her life to future generations."

Brandon watched in fascination as the page began to glow. A picture began to slowly materialize. He saw two teenaged girls, one was kneading dough and the other was extracting honey from a beehive.

"They were my pride and joy," a small, tremulous voice emanated from the journal, and Brandon nearly dropped it. He saw a picture of a beautiful woman. He noticed that her eyes stared blankly and that she carried a long stick that resembled a shepherd's staff. "Jordan? Is she blind? "A picture of Hannah invaded his mind.

"Yes, Brandon. Let her explain."

The voice continued. "After I inhaled the forbidden perfume, I saw unspeakable things I'll never forget. I cried to the Lord to close my eyes forever. He said he could not close my mind's eye, but he would close my physical eyes if that is what I wanted. First, he showed me and my husband what our disobedience had caused.

"Before the Lord banished us from Peace Glen, we lived in natural companionship with him. There was no need for clothes. After our mistake, the Imperial Lord could no longer look upon us without seeing our guilt. He is too pure, you see. He fashioned garments for us from the wool of two sheep. We had to watch as he killed the innocent creatures. He was sobbing the whole time." Evelina's voice shook with sadness. "I've never heard anything like it. I was sobbing, too. When Adamant and I settled in Crimilia, we had two daughters. We always told them that an innocent sacrifice was necessary to cover them.

"After I witnessed the fashioning of the garments, the Lord closed my eyes."

"P-Please, m-m'am?" Brandon stammered. "What happened to your daughters? Which girl is which?"

The voice wavered. "Camilla was a beekeeper. Abigail was a baker. They'd just turned eighteen, and Adamant told them that now was the time to present sacrifices to the Imperial Lord. For their birthday, he gave each of them a newborn lamb. We were farmers, you see. He gave them a week to prepare.

"As the week went by, we noticed that Camilla was absent from the house a great deal. She was often silent and brooding. I asked her what was wrong, and she said she'd been having dreams, but she wouldn't confide in me. All I know is that she became fixated on procuring the perfect nectar to make the best honey. One night, I had a dream."

Brandon saw pictures of the beekeeper following a strange-looking bee. The tips of the insect's wings were golden in color, and it shimmered with a translucent light. The bee alighted upon exquisitely beautiful flowers and gathered nectar. Then the pictures revealed Camilla gathering jars filled with delicious-looking honey. Brandon's mouth watered.

"I knew Camilla was being corrupted in some way just as I had been. The Lord sent me the dream as a sign. I tried to warn her, but she refused to listen." Evelina's voice broke. "She made her choice just as I did.

"The day for the sacrifices arrived." Brandon saw both sisters standing before a flat stone on a hillside. Abigail carried a beautiful white lamb in her arms. She was trembling. Brandon noticed that Camilla carried three jars of honey.

Abigail laid the lamb onto the rock and drew a knife from the pocket of the simple homespun robe she wore. Her face was white and she was crying. Brandon guessed what she was about to do and he lowered his gaze. He trembled.

"It was necessary," Evelina whispered. "Because of me, it was necessary."

After the deed was done, Brandon looked in time to see Abigail build a fire. She fashioned a small, round cake out of flour, sugar, water, and chestnuts and baked it in the flames.

A beautiful white deer appeared out of nowhere. Brandon ascertained that it was a buck because of the gilded antlers. The deer bent low over Abigail's face and gently breathed onto her forehead. Then, he lowered his majestic head and accepted the cake from the trembling girl's hand.

Brandon watched Camilla step forward. He saw Abigail quickly gesture to her cake ingredients. "I have some for you, too, Camilla," she whispered. "Where's your lamb?"

"I don't need one, Abigail," Camilla said. "I've prepared my own work for the Imperial Lord. He will be pleased." So saying, she laid the three jars of honey onto the rock and bowed her head.

The deer looked with sorrowful eyes at the girl then at the honey jars. He stepped backward.

Camilla blinked in shock and anger. "What's wrong?" she asked in disbelief.

"Your lamb, sister," Abigail said gently. "Remember what Mother and Father said? An innocent life is required."

Camilla glared. "I don't need you to lecture me! She said that—"

"Who? What're you talking about?"

Camilla glared and stalked away. Abigail stared after her.

Brandon watched the deer follow Camilla to a clump of rhododendron bushes. "Camilla, my child." Brandon heard no voice, and he was certain Camilla didn't either. The words seemed to transmit themselves into his mind. "Why are you so angry? If you do what is right, you'll be safe. If you do not, a poisoner lies in wait ready to destroy you. Be vigilant."

Camilla looked at the deer with contempt and stalked away. Brandon watched her catapult into a nearby thicket and run headlong into a beautiful scarlet cow. The cow bent its head and gently licked Camilla's hand with a rough-textured tongue. "The work of your hands is essential. He plays favorites. Your sister craves attention." Once again, words seeped into Brandon's mind.

"Your voice is the bee's voice from my dreams," Camilla whispered in awe. "W-What do you want from me?"

"Simply milk me. You'll know what to do from there."

Camilla obeyed. Brandon noticed the milk was watery-looking like the skim milk his mother often bought.

"I'll be with you, though not in this form," the cow whispered. "Go. Do this and you'll be remembered forever."

Trembling, Camilla rushed to the house. Abigail was baking bread.

"Abigail, I'm sorry about earlier. I just overreacted. Can you make me some of your egg custard? I've brought you some milk as a peace offering."

Abigail turned. "There's nothing to forgive, Camilla. Yes, I'll make you some custard."

She took the pail and stared at the watery liquid. "It looks as if it might curdle. I don't think the custard will be good."

"It's safe. I've already tasted it. If you're that nervous, then taste it yourself."

Abigail hesitated and then shrugged. "Well, it can't be any worse than my first attempt at a soufflé!" Grimacing, she took a cupful of the milk.

After she'd finished the cup, she suddenly clutched her chest and fell to the ground. She gasped and began to choke. Brandon screamed as he saw sores erupt onto the young girl's face, arms, and legs.

"Stop it, Jordan! Make it stop!" he covered his eyes, but he couldn't banish the horrific sight. His mind was wrenched back to the fateful day his dad succumbed to pneumonia. Brandon remembered, although he'd been only five at the time, his father's gasps for breath and flushed face.

Jordan quickly closed the book and returned it to the tree. Gently, he caressed Brandon's forehead. "I'm sorry," he whispered. "Do you see now?"

"I think so. Did Abigail die?"

"Yes. The Imperial Lord exiled Camilla to the land of Normdal. Eventually, other children of Adamant and Evelina settled there. Two races were born—one of darkness and one of light. Some of the children chose to follow their parents and listened to the Imperial Lord and others followed Camilla's example.

One night, a serpent bit Camilla as she slept. Then Salak established her rightful place as queen. Even so, there's always a remnant that seeks to do what is right. To protect his people, the Imperial Lord wove his Tapestry of Safety."

Brandon didn't think he could take much more information, but he felt compelled to ask the question. "Tapestry of Safety?"

"Yes. It was woven from the filaments of song and covers our whole land. Evelina's journal recounts how, as the Imperial Lord sang, the melody formed itself into thread. Look above you."

Shielding his eyes from the sun, Brandon obeyed. He could barely glimpse a strange canopy-like substance. As his eyes adjusted to the brilliance, he saw a resplendent picture of multi-colored threads. Brandon blinked in wonder. Vibrant colors dominated the canopy: reds, purples, greens, pinks, and blues. He saw that intricate words were woven into the fabric.

"Has the tapestry always protected you?"

Jordan hesitated. "Look again," he instructed.

As Brandon shifted his focus back to the tapestry, he came to realize that other threads were visible. These threads were also intricate, but they seemed to be made from a coarser material.

"Corruption has come over the years," Jordan explained. "Those who have been appointed to be our overseers have allowed Salak to influence them. She sings her dark melodies, and you can see the result.

"Now, I must show you something else."

Jordan pulled up the sleeve of his camel hair coat. Brandon hobbled forward in order to look. He gasped.

On the man's arm, faded but clearly visible, was a tattoo. The tattoo was crimson in color. It showed a serpent attacking a newborn lamb. The serpent's red fangs were embedded in the lamb's hind hoof.

"Whoa! What is it?" Brandon swallowed.

"The Mark of Allegiance. All of us must wear one. Our first memory as infants is the searing heat of the iron."

"You mean, the queen—"

"Yes, lad. It's the Birthing Ceremony. The Mark of Allegiance stays with us all our lives."

"You mean she watches little babies being branded like cows?" An image of his grandfather's farm flashed through Brandon's mind. He remembered the day he'd held a struggling calf while Grandpa Nick touched the hot iron to the calf's back. The calf had emitted an ear-piercing scream that still haunted Brandon to this day.

"That she does, lad. It's her favorite ceremony. Unless you count the Union one, of course."

"The what?"

Jordan cleared his throat. "Some things are better left unknown. How old are you, Brandon?"

"I'm thirteen. Why?"

Jordan fidgeted nervously. "We'll have to keep you with me for a while. Jamal was right."

"Wait a minute," Brandon said. "Jamal's sleeves were pulled up when you went into the water. I didn't see a Mark of Allegiance on him."

Jordan's face shone like a newly lit candle. "You wouldn't, lad. The iron had no effect on him!"

"What?"

"It's true, the Imperial Lord be praised! My mother, Eliza, recounts the story every chance she gets! Thirty times that iron touched his skin, but it didn't do any good. Salak would have administered it a million times, but I think she saw it was useless."

"Thirty times?" Brandon was thunderstruck. "But his arm would have fallen off! He probably would have needed skin grafts!"

"Skin grafts? I'll never understand you. His arm was not burned. Do you remember the Mirror of Cleansing? Its filth was washed away before it touched the water! Don't you see?"

Brandon opened his mouth to say something when an echoing tramp of footsteps was heard.

Two large men dressed in purple and scarlet suits emerged from a clump of trees. "Jordan Ernest! Son of Zumril and Eliza Ernest! I hereby summon you to the Palace of Herman Zonderman in the Province of Sumril! You're under arrest!" one of the men shouted.

"On what charge?" Jordan asked calmly.

The other man sneered. "You know!" he scoffed. "No one taunts Herman and Hermia and gets away with it!"

"I merely told the truth. Salak rules over Herman and his wife. She sent you, didn't she?"

The other man laughed. "She may have, but that's not the point. You're coming regardless of who sent us." He grabbed Jordan's arms and twisted them behind his back. The other man wound ropes around the silent captive.

"Brandon, young lad!" Jordan called. "Run toward the North! Run toward Jamal! The Imperial Lord protect you!"

"Wait!" Brandon cried. "I can't run very fast! I don't—"

"Crippled lamb will vanquish wicked lioness!" Jordan shouted as he was dragged away.

Brandon stared into space for a moment. *I'll wake up soon! If I don't, I'll check myself into a loony bin!*

Then he began hobbling forward, his stomach leaden with fear.

blind birds and tempting trifles

"And what do you expect me to do, I'd like to know?" Aufeld snapped. "Armand, he just walked in here! I couldn't stop him!"

Armand, a thin man with a weak chin, snorted. "It'll be your head she has, not mine!"

"What can we do? That baker is mad, I tell you!"

"I don't know what Crimilia is coming to. People showing up out of nowhere! By the way, how's that girl you brought in?"

"She's eating right now. Louise is with her." He trembled. "Her Majesty was furious when I told her of the girl's arrival. I've never seen a person's face grow so deathly pale. What can it mean?"

Armand was silent. After a moment, he quoted softly, "Blind girl and crippled boy will bring an end to Evil's story. Baker will prepare Freedom's Bread in his purifying oven."

Aufeld groaned. "You and your riddles, Armand!"

"You've heard those blasted Imperialites! Every time they're brought here they sing that song."

Aufeld turned away. "I'd better see about the girl. Queen Salak wanted to see her after she'd eaten."

He left the room and trudged down the carpeted hallway. Dazzling tapestries and jeweled figurines were visible on every wall and ivory table. Birdcages sat in every available aperture. Music of a piercing sweetness underlain with heart-wrenching sadness came from the cages. Robins, mockingbirds, goldfinches, and other brightly colored birds trilled their notes upon the silent air.

Aufeld stopped at one cage and looked at a robin redbreast. The bird sat on its perch—its sightless eyes glazed, and its wings clipped. Several times, the bird flapped its wings feebly. In another cage, a daring sparrow flew from his perch only to crash against the bars of his prison. The sparrow crumpled into a heap and sang piteously.

Aufeld turned from the pitiful sight and hurried to the door of the infirmary. As on every door in the palace, a carving of a scarlet rose shone brightly. Aufeld trudged through the door and went to a table in the corner of the room.

Hannah sat alone, an untouched plate of bread, cheese, and apples before her.

"You're supposed to have eaten!" he snapped.

"I wanna know where I am, and I wanna know now!"

"That's not up to me to tell you, wench! Now eat up, or I'll have to make you."

"But why? Look, I hafta get home!"

"Where is home? Were you being truthful to Queen Salak?"

"Salak? What kind of name is that, anyway?"

"Her real name is Lucinda, but you address her simply as Your Majesty. Now eat!"

Hannah glared. "That woman who you left me with didn't make me."

"Louise is too soft with the young ones. I'm telling you to eat at once!"

Hannah picked up a slice of apple. As she was about to take a bite, she heard the *tap-tap* sounds of steps approaching from another room.

"Well, you're back, are ya!" the high-pitched voice of Louise screeched. She was a gaunt, hawk-nosed woman with a washed-out expression. Aufeld often wondered if she ever smiled.

"Yes, and I need to speak with you." Aufeld and Louise left the room.

Sighing with relief, Hannah thrust apple slices into her blue jean pockets. She listened closely to make sure that the voices were still talking.

Then, grasping her cane, she grabbed the plate of bread and cheese and tiptoed as quietly as she could out the door. It was easy for her to find the door because she could hear, as she had ever since entering this strange building, the sound of birds singing.

Groping along the wall and swinging her cane, Hannah shuffled toward the sad music. Her cane touched the bottom of a cage, and she stopped walking.

"You're locked up too," she whispered.

Holding out the plate of bread and cheese, she gingerly broke off a piece and stuck it through the bars. The bird within let out a surprised cheep.

"Enjoy," Hannah whispered.

She turned to walk toward the next cage.

Suddenly, she felt her body being jerked forward, but she felt no hand grab her. The plate she held fell from her hand and shattered on the legs of the next cage.

"What's the matter, my dear?" the bell-like voice echoed around her. "Was the food not to your liking? And look, hoarding precious fruit! We can't allow that, now can we?" The voice was not angry but playful in tone.

"Where are you?" Hannah cried out in panic.

"Why, I'm in my throne room, of course. I've been waiting for you to come back to me. I have a job for you."

"I need to get home!" Hannah cried in panic. All dignity vanished as she began to sob hysterically.

"There, now. You're groveling!" The queen's voice was amused. "I'll help you, but you must help me, first."

"H-Help you?" Hannah stammered.

"Why, yes. You'll be quite safe here. I just need you to open your heart to me. I think I know someone who can help you regain your sight."

"What's wrong with you people!" Hannah screamed. "I'm never going to see again! Leave me alone!"

"Ah, you can't see because you were in an accident in those curious contraptions you call cars. Is that right?"

Hannah sucked in her breath. "Yes," she whispered. "How did you know?"

"I see more than you think. Your mother was driving your fifth-grade class to an amusement park. She hit a tree. You hit your head, and a boy, Brandon, suffered a spinal injury. Correct?"

Tears flowed unchecked from Hannah's eyes. "Yes," she said.

"Your father left shortly after the accident. Correct?"

Hannah swallowed. "Yes."

"I can introduce you to someone who can help you. Your mother would no longer have to work to pay doctor's bills. She could be home when you finished school, and she could wake you up in the morning. Come, help me by letting me help you."

Hannah hesitated for a moment. "What can I do?"

"Just lean forward. I'll transport you to my throne room and give you something special to build up your strength. The food I offer is more substantial than apples and bread. Tomorrow, I'll show you the person who can help you."

Hannah hesitated for only a moment more. A vision of her mother invaded her mind. Mom cried at night. Hannah had heard her often. She nodded and leaned forward. She held out her arms.

Something like a caressing breeze lifted her off the ground. She felt as if she were floating on a cloud.

After a few moments, she felt herself being lowered onto a soft couch. A bowl filled with a fragrant soup was placed into her hands.

"Lamb's broth," Salak's voice intoned. "Drink it all, and then sleep. Things will look better in the morning."

Hannah placed the bowl to her lips and began to pour the liquid down her throat. The broth was sweet and spicy, pungent with onions and garlic. After a few ladylike sips, Hannah began guzzling hungrily. She'd never tasted anything with so much flavor!

After the broth, Salak proffered a heart-shaped box. "Trifles of Inertia. They're pure heaven. Try one."

Hannah reached forward to grab a morsel, but her hands were too heavy. Her eyes felt weighted down.

"Do you want me to feed you?" Salak asked kindly.

In her dazed stupor, Hannah managed to nod her head. She felt round, chocolate-covered morsels being gently placed in her mouth.

Hannah gasped at the sweetness of the taste: orange creams, marzipan, and hazelnut chocolates were pushed down her throat so rapidly she couldn't distinguish one taste from another. However, she relished the pure ecstasy of the sweet mixture.

In a few moments, Hannah became so dazed she could no longer think. She fell back onto the silken couch into nothingness.

a taste of joy

Brandon stumbled forward in the darkness. Owls hooted from nearby trees, and his limbs were heavy and sluggish. Sighing, he approached a cherry tree and leaned against its rough bark.

Twelve hours had passed since Jordan had been arrested. Brandon had walked steadily in the direction he'd seen Jamal walk. He was still at a loss as to what to do. Even if he found Jamal, what could he tell him? For perhaps the hundredth time, he berated himself for not retrieving Evelina's journal.

Well, at least he hadn't gone hungry! As Jordan had left, he'd managed to throw his pouch to the ground. The pouch held grasshoppers, willow bark, and some berries. Not the most appetizing meals, but Brandon was managing.

Brandon picked a few cherries off the tree and placed them in the pouch. He was about to move forward again when he heard a rumbling peal of thunder. Great! Just great!

After a few moments, large drops of rain began to pelt his skin. He struggled onward, knowing that he couldn't seek shelter under the trees. Jagged bolts of lightning sliced through the sky.

"You! Boy! What're ya doin' out here?" A rumbling voice echoed around him.

Brandon jumped and strained his eyes looking for the speaker. Soon, he saw a muscular woman silhouetted in the entrance of a log hut. She wore a black homespun robe, and her voice was raspy.

"What this world's comin' to, I don't know! My Mendel's asleep in there, but I heard the most peculiar noise! Ya best come in here for the night!"

"But, I need to find—"

"My stars, boy! Ya won't get far in this weather! Now come on in!"

Brandon followed the large woman into the small hut. "Ya look a mite famished. I got some bread and apples. Will that do?" the woman inquired.

Brandon's stomach growled. His mouth watered, and he nodded his thanks.

"Sit yourself down, then. Name's Ursula, by the way! Ursula Maloney."

"Brandon Pringle," he said, plunking himself down on a wooden bench.

The room was filled with makeshift gardening tools and fishing equipment. Ursula noticed Brandon looking "River Pridar's 'bout a day's walk from here.

We want meat, we gotta get it ourselves! Mendel goes fishing whenever he gets a chance. With these blasted taxes, we have to make do the best we can. The Imperial Lord provides, but *phew*! I'm gettin' mighty tired!"

"Taxes?"

"They go up every month. Soon we'll all starve." Ursula placed a slice of bread and an apple in front of her guest. "The bread's the best you'll find anywhere. Baked by Jamal himself!"

"Jamal?" Brandon spoke sharply. "That's who I'm looking for."

"You don't say! Why?"

Brandon opened his mouth, but Ursula spoke first. "Ah! You want your leg fixed. Is that it?"

"What?"

"That's right. He can fix anything! I've seen him heal a paralyzed woman with me own eyes!"

Brandon was too stunned to speak. Instead, he bit into the bread. His eyes opened wide in astonishment. The bread was crusty and spicy on the outside and silky and sweet inside. He tasted honey and a hint of olive oil, a combination that was surprisingly good. He'd never tasted anything so extraordinary!

Ursula smiled. "He's a regular wizard when he cooks! You should try his pastries! But now he's left home for something else, said he had to tell others that freedom was near! Can you imagine? He could be rich, but no! His brother, Marshall, was plenty mad!"

Brandon was half listening to Ursula's prattle. A feeling of euphoria and peace flooded through him. He felt comforted and strengthened.

"I haven't felt so good in a while," he said.

"Ah! You feel it too, eh?"

"Yeah. Where's that feeling coming from?"

"Anything that man touches is blessed. I don't understand it any more than you do. No one understands Jamal completely. No one ever has."

"I heard his mother's name is Marigold. Where does she live?"

"Oh, not too far from here. She's quite a woman. I've known her since she was a young girl, and the hardships she's been through!"

"What do you mean?"

"When she was nearly fourteen, people found out she was gonna have a baby! *Phew!* The scandal!"

"Who was the father?"

"She claims the Imperial Lord is Jamal's father! Poor Joakim was plenty surprised, I can tell ya!"

"Who's Joakim?"

"Joakim was the baker. He was engaged to Marigold, and he considered breaking it off."

"What happened?"

"Well, you're not gonna believe it, but he claimed that Marigold was telling the truth; said he had some sort of dream! Queen Salak was plenty mad! Here Marigold was of age, and she hadn't attended the Union Ceremony!"

"I heard about that. What exactly is it?"

"My stars, child! Ya don't wanna know!"

Brandon was silent for a moment. He bit into an apple slice as he thought, *Is she trustworthy?*

Finally, he spoke, "I met Jamal's cousin, Jordan, at Pridar River. He's been taken."

Ursula turned white, but her face didn't register surprise. "I knew he would, sooner or later! He's always speaking against Herman and Hermia! Did he think they'd let it slide?"

"What's he say about them?"

"Well, um, it's complicated. King Herman of Sumril has married Hermia, his brother's wife. Philip is still alive, and Jordan says that Herman and Hermia are servants of the False Reflector. He claims that they have sinned."

"Well, anyway, I hafta find Jamal. Maybe he can do something."

Ursula's face hardened. "Jamal and Jordan should have stayed at their homes and done their jobs! They've caused no end of trouble for us!"

"Ursula!" A rumbling voice erupted in the darkness. "You talk so freely! Hold your tongue!"

A huge man suddenly rose up from a cot in the corner. His shaggy beard fell to his chest, and he wore a black robe. "Young man!" he thundered. "We're simple folk here. What's your business with us?"

"Ah, lay off him, Mendel! The poor lad's plumb worn out," Ursula snapped. "Get on back to bed will ya!"

Mendel grunted and stood up. "Since you're up blabbin' secrets, ya might as well give me some bread!" he grumbled.

"All right, but we're runnin' low." Ursula cut a slice, and Mendel plopped down beside Brandon. The bench creaked ominously. "Well, young one. So you know Jordan, do ya?"

"Yes, sir, and Jamal too. They're different, but they seem nice."

"Nice?" Mendel grunted. He'd taken a bite of bread, and his grumpy demeanor was disappearing. He still spoke brusquely, but his face had softened. "Nice is one thing they're not! They're honest and uncompromising. They are the instruments of love itself. Nice doesn't have anything to do with it."

"I don't understand."

Mendel smiled for the first time. "Jamal's the Imperial Lord's instrument. He doesn't care about popularity. Jordan's always been outspoken, and he wants people to follow his cousin."

"What do they plan to do?"

Mendel grinned. "Vanquish Salak, of course! The Imperial Lord be praised!"

"And you tell me to hold my tongue," Ursula scoffed.

"I know most of the story but not the beginning. Why were Adamant and Evelina banished from Peace Glen? Why is Salak still ruling? Nobody I've met here seems to like her. Couldn't the Imperial Lord banish her?"

"Plenty of people like what she offers. As to her right to rule, the Imperial Lord had no choice."

"What happened?"

Ursula and Mendel looked at one another. Finally, Mendel sighed. "I'll tell you, boy. But first, I must look at your left arm."

Brandon guessed the reason, and he rolled up his sleeve. Mendel smiled when he saw the clear flesh. "Very good, lad," he murmured.

Holding up his own left arm, Mendel instructed Brandon to look. The Mark of Allegiance was faded but still visible. Mendel nodded to Ursula, who showed her own arm.

"But both of you have the mark," Brandon pointed out in confusion.

"It's all in how you look at things," Ursula said. She pointed to her forehead. Mendel bent forward and pointed to his as well.

Brandon peered closely. A rectangular picture could be seen of an old-fashioned brick oven, the kind used at Boy Scout camp when cooking over an open flame.

Brandon was totally bewildered. "An oven?" he cried. "What does that mean?"

Mendel explained. "It's all about the Imperial Lord's poetic justice. The first crime involved the murder of a baker, so the prophecies tell of a baker who will prepare Freedom's Bread. Those who claim to know say the prophecies are symbolic, but no matter how you look at them, the truth is clear. The price of true freedom is tremendous pain."

"So you mean this picture was branded onto your foreheads with the iron too?"

Ursula smiled. "Oh no, lad! We're Imperialites. Our Lord does not inflict suffering."

"Then what—"

"Someone is coming who must suffer for us," Mendel explained. "Make yourself as comfortable as you can. This story will take a while."

a fallen princess, a fabulous promise

"He's here?" Salak's face, usually pale, glowed crimson with excitement.

"Yes, my queen," Aufeld said. "He's in the dungeon as you ordered."

Salak smiled. She rose from her throne, her silk dress billowing around her. At the door, she turned back. "Aufeld?"

"My queen?"

"On no account am I to be disturbed!"

Aufeld nodded as his queen withdrew.

Strolling leisurely, Salak made her way past numerous doors and passages. As she passed the birdcages, she paused to sneer at the imprisoned creatures. "Did he cry when he saw you?" she asked a mockingbird. The bird's only answer was a chirp of fright. Salak laughed and continued on her way.

In a dank cell, Jamal lay huddled on the cold floor. His lips moved in silent conversation. Often, he stared at his callused hands. "Father, be with me. Give me strength," he prayed.

"So, you did come," a familiar voice rang out. "Welcome."

Jamal looked up into the leering face of his foe. "You knew I would come," he stated matter-of-factly.

Salak leaned forward. She peered into the window of Jamal's cell. "I thought your loving father would spare you from this part of the journey. After all, you'll meet me again soon enough," she grinned.

"Go ahead and do what you came to do," Jamal said sharply.

Salak's face clouded. "I can't do what I'd like to," she snarled. "Not yet, anyway!"

Then her face softened. She turned to a table behind her where an array of pastries, breads, and cakes were sitting on a jeweled platter. The cakes were covered in frostings of brilliant colors: pink, violet, red, and yellow. Salak selected a particularly large cake covered in rainbow sprinkles and pink frosting. She sank brilliant white teeth into the confection. Raspberry jam oozed from between her teeth and covered her lips. Her scarlet tongue licked the syrupy jam away. It was like watching a carnivore devour a choice piece of raw meat.

"You must be hungry. Have you eaten today?" she asked tauntingly. She grabbed another cake and crammed it into her mouth.

"No," Jamal said tonelessly. His mouth watered. He turned away.

"Ah! That's right! You're fasting. A shame, really." She gestured to the platter of sweets. "They'll just go to waste if you don't indulge."

Jamal didn't answer.

Salak smiled. She reached into a pocket of her dress and withdrew a flat stone. "On the other hand," she said musingly, "you're the Imperial Lord's son!" Her words dripped with sarcasm. "Why, you could easily change this stone into a whole roomful of pastries. Think of those who serve you! They'd definitely follow someone with such talent and power!"

Jamal stared at the stone Salak clutched in her hand. "It is written in the Tapestry of Safety, 'People do not live on merely food. They are nourished by The Imperial Lord's wisdom.'"

Salak smiled knowingly and shrugged. "Very well," she said. "I'll just leave this stone with you, shall I? And the pastries too. Surely there can be no harm in satisfying hunger."

She turned away as if to leave. Then she turned back. "By the way, I have a reliable source that informs me your cousin is languishing in King Herman's prison. What a shame! If you weren't so stubborn, you could be free to deliver him, but I'm afraid you must remain where you are for the time being. I'll see you tomorrow," she grinned.

Jamal listened to the retreating footsteps. Just as they were about to fade away, he called, "Salak?"

The queen of Crimilia turned. "Do you ever miss being in my father's service?" His voice held a note of sadness.

The question cut into her mind like a sharp knife. She glared. "The name's Lucinda! I serve no one but myself!"

As she stamped away, Salak's lip trembled. He always managed to ask just the question that forced her to remember her past. That fake concern! It had to be an act! No one could care about anyone or anything as much as he pretended! The nerve of him!

In her throne room, she snatched her mirror. Peering into its depths, she demanded, "Show me Peace Glen!"

The mirror clouded, then an image of a magnificent garden filled with fruit trees, flowers, lush meadows, and pristine waterfalls appeared. Two dazzling winged creatures stood guard at the glen's entrance. They held flaming swords.

Salak stared at the enthralling vision as memories invaded her mind.

Her first memory had been of glorious music, a swelling symphony of ascending beauty. Gradually, she realized that the music was coming from three dazzlingly brilliant Presences—beings who were distinct yet linked together. Soon she came to learn that the beings were the Imperial Lord, His Son, and the pure alurian, or Spirit.

In her memory, they hovered over her prostrate form, bathing her in an overwhelming light. A feeling like nothing she could describe overflowed within her.

"The feeling is called joy," the Imperial Lord's Son said.

In the reflection the Presences cast, she caught a glimpse of herself. Dazzling light poured from her like a fountain, and her face shone as brilliantly as a freshly cultivated pearl.

"Is this light coming from you, or can I make it myself?" she'd asked, genuinely awed and entranced by the image.

"Both," the Imperial Lord explained. "You are distinct from us, yet you are a part of us."

The Eternal Presences had created her, a being more beautiful than any ever made before: an Eaglia princess. Eaglias were message bearers and worshippers of the Imperial Lord. They were shape shifters and had the ability to fly when necessary. Lucinda was the most beautiful Eaglia of all.

All the Eaglias were given specific talents and gifts, and they each had specific duties to perform. Lucinda's greatest gifts were those of music and oratory. When she spoke, she entranced others with her extraordinary voice.

She'd witnessed the creation of all things and remembered with vivid clarity how the Eternal Presences worked together. They'd performed an intricate dance of such beauty it was indescribable. As they danced and shouted commands, every object they mentioned appeared. The dancing grew more and more magnificent until the Presences merged into one to create their masterpiece.

As the dance progressed, all the Eaglias sang an accompanying music of joy. Lucinda's voice rose above all others. Lucinda sang in jubilation with the rest of His creation as the Presences made mankind.

"Humans are made as a mirror reflection of our inner being! They will provide us with the gift of worship and care for our creation. The first man will be named Adamant, and the first woman will be named Evelina."

"Lucinda, gift giver and bearer of brilliance, we entrust these humans to you. Teach them the art of music and craftsmanship. Be a companion and mentor to them."

And she did just that.

Each day, the Imperial Lord, His Son, and the Alurian came down to Peace Glen to spend time with Adamant and Evelina. They walked with the man and woman and shared meals with them. Adamant and Evelina always fashioned gifts for their creators from the riches that surrounded them. Lucinda watched this friendship and marveled that such superior beings exhibited such overwhelming love for their creation.

After some time, Lucinda's own breathtaking image wouldn't leave her mind. She began to wonder, *Why should only the Imperial Lord and his Son be worshiped? Aren't I just as important as them? After all, I have a*

responsibility to care for the man and woman. Shouldn't I be revered in return?

In the center of Peace Glen, there grew two rosebushes: one shimmered with dazzlingly white blooms, the other contained scarlet roses of an immense brightness. "The white roses are the Roses of Youth and Eternity, and the red roses are the Roses of Revelation. You may enjoy any flower but the ones from the crimson rosebush." The Imperial Lord had instructed Adamant and Evelina, "On the day you inhale the perfume from the Roses of Revelation, you will die."

Lucinda watched the Imperial Lord instructing the man and woman about the flowers. The mask of her dazzling features briefly fell away, revealing distorted ugliness. The flower of pride had finally burst into full bloom, and its poison was doing its destructive work. The joy that she'd experienced for so long had withered, and now a new feeling materialized. Her own mind furnished the word for this feeling: jealousy.

One morning, when Peace Glen was awash in pearly-bright dew, Lucinda approached the woman. Evelina sat by a crystal pool and gathered honeysuckle flowers. A lion and leopard sat beside her, and she often paused in her work to stroke their heads. The sunlight glinted on her chestnut hair and bare shoulders, and her emerald green eyes sparkled with happiness.

Lucinda and Evelina loved to converse. They laughed and enjoyed each other's company all the time. They discussed music and beauty.

Lucinda wore a dress of apricot-colored silk covered in jewels. "Evelina! You're looking quite well today! Tell me, where's Adamant?"

"He's gone to gather some grapes." She peered closely at her friend's beautiful gown. "Lucinda, why have you covered yourself? You look different, somehow."

"I have advanced in my service to the Imperial Lord. This is his reward to me," Lucinda lied.

Evelina nodded and smiled. "He provides so much, doesn't he? Aren't we blessed?"

Lucinda laughed in delight. "Of course, but tell me. There's a rumor circulating among the Eaglias. Did the Imperial Lord really say you mustn't look at any flower in Peace Glen nor inhale the perfume from them? That seems such a strange rule! I mean, the flowers are breathtakingly beautiful!"

Evelina laughed in disbelief. "That's a good joke, Lucinda! Where did you get your information? Of course we can enjoy the flowers." Then she hesitated. "There is one rosebush in the center of Peace Glen. The Imperial Lord did say we must not inhale the perfume from the Rosebush of Revelation nor should we touch it, or we would die."

Salak smiled to herself as she recalled the memory. The dumb cow hadn't even gotten his commandment right! The plan would work beautifully!

She sat down beside Evelina, her exquisite dress fluttering as she did so. "You know I respect the Imperial Lord as much as you do, but he's wrong about that rosebush."

"Wrong? What are you talking—?"

"Oh! Please don't misunderstand me. Maybe he's just jealous."

"Jealous? What is that?"

"It simply means that he wants all the power. You see, Evelina, you shall surely not die if you inhale the perfume from that rosebush."

Evelina gasped. "How do you know?"

"Because I've smelled it myself. The Imperial Lord knows that when you breathe in the rose's fragrance, you'll become like him. You'll know all things, both the things that are good and the things that are evil."

"What is evil?"

Lucinda did not enlighten her. She changed the subject and discussed opera and other kinds of music. As she talked, Evelina slipped away.

Salak quivered in delight as she remembered transforming into a serpent for the first time: the joy of stretching and coiling! In this form, she could observe people without being noticed.

She watched in delight as Evelina stood before the brilliant rosebush. The scarlet flowers seemed to quiver in anticipation. In her serpent form, she wound around the woman's legs.

"Be wise and grow in knowledge," she crooned.

Evelina laughed in delight. "Oh, Lucinda! How beautiful you look! I love to watch you change into other creatures! Now change into a butterfly! They're my favorite!"

Evelina then turned back to the rosebush. She stared transfixed a few minutes longer. *What would it be like to rule all things, to know everything?*

At long last, she leaned forward and inhaled the intoxicating perfume of the Rose of Revelation.

Salak remembered the look of euphoria that briefly passed over the woman's face. In that moment, she struck with her serpent fangs, piercing the white skin of Evelina's leg.

The woman cried out in sudden horror as the realization of her action hit her. She stared in fright at the scarlet snake and then began to sob. "It was a lie! I'm nothing like him! Why, Lucinda? I—" Evelina crumpled to the ground, her voice trailing away. Lucinda cast one look of triumph onto her former friend and slithered away into dewy grass.

Lucinda watched Evelina writhe in anguish. The lion and leopard approached the woman, looked at her, then bolted away in panic. Evelina's cries of anguish and fear increased.

With a flurry of wings, a snow-white dove fluttered down and alighted by Evelina's side. "Alurian, Great Spirit, I'm sorry!" Evelina gasped. "Please, take this pain away! I—she made me—"

The dove looked at her with sorrow. Amber tears drenched his white plumage. In his beak was clutched a white rose petal from the Rosebush of Eternity. Gently, he let the tear-stained petal fall onto the snake bite.

The petal affixed itself to the wound, and Lucinda heard a hissing sound as her venom was drained away. The wound closed, and the petal fluttered to the ground, brown and lifeless.

Lucinda heard the dove's words as if he were speaking aloud. "I cannot take the pain away, Evelina. The roses of Eternity are no longer available to you. You must leave here."

The dove flew away. As Evelina staggered to her feet, Adamant suddenly appeared holding a cluster of grapes. His finely-chiseled features grew ashen when he saw his wife's face. Dropping the fruit, he ran to her and enfolded her into his arms.

Now Salak recalled how she'd watched Evelina plead with Adamant to join her. "I've done wrong, but I can't bear to be left alone!"

They cried and clung to one another. After a while, the man followed his wife's example.

"Now, they have become like us," Lucinda heard Father and Son talking together. Indescribable pain throbbed in their speech. "Yet they are only human. We cannot allow them to inhale the perfume from the Roses of Eternity. They can't live forever with the knowledge they have acquired. Life would be nothing but despair for them."

The son shifted his all-knowing radiance onto the eavesdropping Eaglia. Terrifying anger seemed to emanate from him.

With a blinding flash, Lucinda was hurled into nothingness. "You're name is now Salak, deformer and poisoner!" the Imperial Lord's voice thundered.

She'd landed in a parched desert, isolated and empty.

"You can't banish me!" she'd fumed. "I have a right of ownership! They listened to me, and I told them what they wanted to hear!"

"Yes, my fair princess," the Imperial Lord's voice, choked with sobs, echoed in the darkness, "but your right to rule will not last forever. I will cause hostility to form between you and the woman. A pure deliverer will arise from her seed who will crush you into powder under his feet. Though you crush him for a time, he will rise again to vanquish you! Because of her guilt, Evelina requested that her physical eyes be closed. I have allowed this; not to shame her, but to give her hope. The loss of her sight will serve as a reminder that I will avenge the molestation which you brought upon her. I will use two individuals whom you perceive as weak to complete your downfall. 'Blind girl and crippled boy will bring an end to Evil's story.'"

"We'll see." Salak smiled with contempt. "With the regulations I'll enforce, your precious seed will be corrupted and defiled! Weaklings will never vanquish me!"

The Imperial Lord had not bothered to answer. His voice had faded away.

In her winged form, Salak flew to Crimilia, the borderland of Peace Glen where Adamant and Evelina now lived. After biding her time for eighteen long years, she established her rule over Evelina, Adamant, and their offspring, forcing them to wear the Mark of Allegiance. The Mark passed from generation to generation. Salak also enforced the Union Ceremony.

Now, she leaned back with a smile of satisfaction. Jamal was in her dungeon. All would be well by and by.

the market

"So you see, lad," Mendel boomed, "Salak must rule until the Deliverer comes."

Brandon nodded although he was still a little confused. His head was reeling with all the information he'd learned.

"But what can I do? Why am I here?" he murmured to himself.

"It is a mystery, lad," Ursula said. "Strange things are happening all the time around here."

"You can come with me tomorrow, if you like," Mendel said. "I have to go to the market in Nunmal to distribute vegetables. Not that there's much to distribute! On the way back, we'll stop at Marigold's house."

"You're welcome to stay here for the night," Ursula said.

Brandon nodded his thanks, and Ursula rose to fetch a blanket. "I'm afraid that bench is the only other place for sleeping," she called.

"No problem," Brandon said. "Thanks for the food."

The next morning dawned bright with sunlight. After Brandon and Mendel had eaten one small slice of bread apiece, they left the hut.

Mendel loaded three burlap sacks of vegetables onto a makeshift cart. "You can sit in the cart if you'd like, lad. It's a long walk."

Brandon shook his head. "We'll take turns. How's that?"

Mendel shrugged. "That's up to you, lad. Just don't tire yourself."

The two companions set out. Brandon pushed the cart for a while but quickly realized that his leg was not yet strong enough to handle the strain of the load. It wasn't long before Mendel had to take over.

When the sun reached the center of the sky, Mendel and Brandon entered a village square. The noise was deafening, and enormous crowds rushed in every direction.

"Whoa! What a place!" Brandon peered at men, women, and children who carried armloads of packages. The people jostled each other in their frenzied activity. Vendors called from booths packed high with food, tools, and other merchandise. Brandon's eyes strayed to their cart with the pitiful supplies of vegetables.

Mendel frowned. "This is the marketplace of self-absorption," he murmured. "Look at the crowd closely."

Brandon did so and saw that the people were not looking at one another. They acknowledged no one.

Brandon noticed a woman approach a spice merchant. Wordlessly, she pointed to a package of dill. The man in the booth barked: "Proof before purchase!" The woman held out her left arm. Brandon gasped in astonishment. Although he'd seen the Mark of Allegiance three times before, he'd never seen it shine with such lividness! The scarlet serpent stood out in blinding brilliance, dwarfing the picture of the suffering lamb.

The man nodded, and the woman handed him a few copper coins. The man gave her the package of dill. She slipped away as quickly as she had come.

"Let's find a place to set out our produce," Mendel said.

Brandon's stomach growled. "Can't we find some food first?" He gestured toward a soup vendor's booth from which the tantalizing aroma of onions, tomatoes, and garlic wafted. He thought how wonderful a plate of his mother's spaghetti would be right now.

Mendel snorted. "Here? No, lad. We can't. Ursula's packed us some food."

Brandon sighed. "Why can't we buy food?"

"Why do you think?" Mendel snapped. Then his voice softened. "Did the woman you saw with the spice merchant not give you a clue?"

Brandon frowned. "But you have the Mark. "

Mendel sighed with impatience. "It's useless to me. I wear a different mark, now, and the queen knows."

"How does she know?"

"Her Mirror of Revelation. She made it herself, and it shows her everyone she desires to see."

"How do you get seeds to plant for vegetables if you can't buy them?"

"Eaglias," Mendel said. "Every month, they bring enough supplies to sustain us. They deliver them to Marigold's hut. We don't get five-course meals, but we have just enough."

"If the Mark of Allegiance is useless, why is it still on your arm?"

"To remind me of where I've come from. Now, do you want lunch?"

Brandon nodded, and he and Mendel shared a meal of apples and bread.

After eating, Mendel pushed the cart to a remote location. Brandon was about to ask why, but he thought better of it.

He helped Mendel arrange small stacks of vegetables. They looked drab and unimpressive when compared with the brightly colored produce of the other booths.

For hours, it seemed that no one would come. At last, a small group of thin, pale children appeared. They were dressed in plain robes, and their faces were pinched with fatigue. The hopelessness in their eyes made Brandon wince.

"Hello there, Melissa," Mendel said pleasantly. "What do you need today?"

"Some corn and beans, please," a brown-haired girl murmured.

Mendel handed her some vegetables.

"Tell your mother that I plan to have some bread to give away next time I come—some of Jamal's bread."

Melissa's eyes lit up, and the other children gasped in delight. "Jamal's bread? Really?" they cried.

"That's right. Now, who's next?"

Soon the small stacks of vegetables had dwindled away, and the children had left with lighter spirits.

Mendel frowned as he watched them depart. "Are you ready, lad?"

Brandon was more than ready. They left the market and rode deeper into the village of Nunmal.

"Marigold lives on Trimland Hill. It's not too far from here."

Soon Mendel stopped the cart before a hut that was almost identical to his own. The only difference was an extra room attached to the back.

Mendel noticed Brandon looking. "That is Jamal's bakery."

A slender woman in a white robe rushed out of the hut. "Mendel! You've come!" the woman cried in delight. She had shoulder-length red hair and hazel eyes. Brandon could see that she was beautiful, but her face was careworn. She looked weary.

"Hello, Marigold," Mendel said. "I have someone for you to meet. This is Brandon."

Marigold stared in wonder. "It's you!" she cried in ecstasy. "You've come!"

Brandon's face turned red with embarrassment. "What do you—"

"Oh, I didn't mean to confuse you. I'll tell you later. Come on in and refresh yourselves."

As Brandon followed Mendel into the hut, he noticed a lightening of his spirits. Although he couldn't explain it, he seemed to feel the lingering presence of love here. For the first time in this strange world, he felt at home.

hannah's task

"Rise and shine," a familiar voice called.

Hannah groaned. She sat up shakily. Her head throbbed. "W-Where am I?" she whispered through chapped lips. Her voice was barely audible.

"You're safe here. I've brought you some breakfast. You have a job to do today, and you need your strength." The disembodied voice faded away, and Hannah heard the clunk of a breakfast tray hit a table on her right side. The familiar smell of pancakes, bacon, and maple syrup filled the air. Hannah's stomach rumbled. Odd. She hadn't felt hungry until the tray appeared.

Feverishly, she groped until she found the tray. She grabbed a forkful of syrup-drenched pancakes and took a bite. Syrup and butter oozed thickly over her tongue. She took a large bite of crunchy bacon.

I don't understand this place, she thought, *but this food's better than oatmeal!*

After she had eaten, she rose shakily and used her cane to explore the room. There wasn't much to discover. A wardrobe was in the corner, and a table and chair stood before it.

Suddenly, the bedroom door opened with a bang. The swishing sound of a silk dress accompanied hurried footsteps. "Ah. You've finished eating. Excellent," the queen said. "How do you feel this morning?"

Hannah turned toward the voice. "Sick," she admitted.

"That's understandable. That bump on your head is quite startling. You will probably have to remain here for several more days. Now, are you ready to hear your task?"

Hannah plopped down on the bed. She didn't feel like doing anything, but she knew that protesting would get her nowhere. "Yes," she said.

"You must take a tray of food to my dungeon. There's a man there who is a prisoner. He is the person I told you about."

Hannah felt her heart begin a rapid tumult. Anticipation filled her soul but was quickly replaced with doubt. "All right," she said.

"Good. Come along with me."

Hannah took her cane and followed the queen out of the room. All around her, she heard the chirping of birds. The floor of the palace was carpeted in some soft material. The soothing scent of lavender filled the air.

"We'll stop by the scullery to get the tray," Salak said.

Focusing on the rustling of the queen's silk gown, Hannah followed close behind. There were so many twists and turns down multiple corridors that she began to feel dizzy.

After what seemed like forever, the pair turned left. Hannah heard the sounds of clattering dishes and a cacophony of voices talking all at once.

Queen Salak's dress rustled as she swept into the tumultuous scullery. Hannah followed close behind. The chatter stopped immediately.

"Griselda? Is the tray prepared?" Salak demanded.

A small voice, barely above a whisper, spoke. "Yes, my queen."

Salak picked up the tray and handed it to Hannah. "Now, the door to the dungeon is on your right. There are five steps that lead downstairs. I'll watch to make sure you reach the bottom safely."

Hannah nodded. Carefully, she used her cane to locate the first step. She clutched the tray and inched her way down the steps. The steps were steeper than she'd anticipated, and several times, she nearly stumbled.

Hannah became aware of the utter stillness the farther down she descended. The only sound was the occasional *drip-drip* of water.

At last, she reached the bottom. Sighing with relief, she inched forward. There was a wall on her right, and she stayed close to it as she tiptoed. Her feet made hollow shuffling sounds that echoed on the marble floor, and her cane scraped loudly along. If the man she was seeking had been asleep, she'd probably woken him up by now.

After five minutes, the wall curved to the right. Hannah turned and continued her slow progress. The silence was frightening.

Suddenly, her cane clanged against a metal door. Hannah cried out in fear. Feverishly, she began to grope along the wall with the back of the hand that held the cane. She felt a doorknob and a small pane of glass. Then she found a small wooden table. Thank goodness! She plopped down the tray.

The sound of movement made her jump, and she nearly dropped her cane.

"Hello," a deep voice said. The voice was gentle, and she noticed it was weak.

"Um, I, uh, brought your breakfast," she managed to say.

"She knows I will not eat. It's useless," the man answered. "How are you, Hannah?"

Hannah suddenly felt lightheaded. She leaned against the wall for support. "What's going on here?" she demanded. "How do you know my name?"

The man didn't answer. Instead, he said, "What did she send you here to ask of me?"

Hannah hesitated. Then she decided to tell the truth. "She says you can help me."

The man didn't speak. Hannah waited for a long moment. A lump rose in her throat.

"She says you can—" she swallowed "—she says—"

"Do you believe I can restore your sight?" the man asked gently.

Tears filled Hannah's eyes. "No," she finally admitted. "The doctors say it's hopeless."

The man nodded in understanding. "Whom do you blame for the accident?"

The question was so unexpected that Hannah was taken aback. She could not speak.

"You do not have to answer me if you do not want to," the man said. "I will not force you to receive my help. Just know I will be here if you ever want to talk."

Hannah stood by the cell door shaking with pain. She felt exposed and frightened.

"You have done your job. Now you may leave if you wish. If you decide to come again, my name is Jamal." His voice was sorrowful.

Hannah began to run away. In the silence, she suddenly heard wracking sobs issuing from Jamal's cell. Surprisingly, it wasn't pity that rose within her but anger. She turned back toward the sound of weeping.

"I blame God, that's who!" she shouted. Then, she stumbled away.

"Salak!" Jamal screamed when the footsteps had faded, "Leave me in peace!" A shadow detached itself from the opposite wall of the dungeon and slithered across the floor. The scarlet serpent coiled herself around the metal grating of the door. Her bulbous, yellow eyes glittered with malicious pleasure.

"You see?" she hissed. "She hates you! She'll serve me now. I must say I'm disappointed. Why not use your father's power to heal her? Prove you're the Imperial Lord's Son!"

"You know why. It was cruel to toy with her emotions! She's vulnerable. It is written: 'You shall not test the Imperial Lord's power for your own purposes.'"

Salak laughed. "What do I care about vulnerability? I'll see you again tomorrow." Changing back into her human form, she glided away into the darkness.

In the hallway, Hannah stood still as a statue. Anger washed through her as she thought about the strange man. Why did he have to ask such personal questions? She remembered the diagnosis of Doctor Franklin and her mother's wail of pain.

Footsteps approached. "Well done, my dear," the musical voice of Salak rang out. "I gather the man could not heal you?"

"He said he would not," Hannah said. She did not feel like going into details.

"He is a strange person. He helps only certain people. Others he leaves to languish in their pain. Now, since you must remain here for a while, I will assign a task for you. You will work in the scullery alongside Griselda. She has been in my service for six years, and she will help you. You will be responsible for washing dishes, churning butter, and baking bread."

"But I need to get home right away!"

Salak smiled. "All in good time. The scullery is the next door on your right. Go in and begin work."

Sighing, Hannah entered the bustling room. The clattering of pots and pans could be heard over many voices.

"Um, I was told to report here," she called.

A hand touched her shoulder. "Hello, miss. I'm Griselda Perkins. Her Majesty told me to instruct you."

"Yes, thanks," Hannah said. "What do I do?"

"Take my hand."

"It's better if I take your arm just above the elbow," Hannah said.

Griselda chuckled timidly. "Um, why?"

"That way, you can walk ahead of me, and I can follow."

"You're different. I've never met anyone without sight. Babies with birth defects are killed. What happened?"

Hannah shuddered, but she thought she'd better not ask what Griselda meant. She didn't want to know. Quickly changing the subject, she asked: "How did you come here, and how old are you?"

"I'm sixteen summers. I came here like you did."

"Like me?"

"Of course, miss. The way we all come here."

"I was riding to school on the bus and—"

"Bus? What is a bus?"

Hannah sighed in exasperation. "A bus helps you get to places. It's quicker than walking."

"Oh! A carriage."

"Something like that." Hannah smiled in spite of herself.

"I came here in a carriage too. So did Madeleine."

"Hold your tongue, Gris!" a harsh voice shouted

"Ah! Lighten up, Madeleine. She's a new worker. She's supposed to bake bread and wash dishes."

"Ha! She gets the easy work, of course!" Madeleine snapped.

"Don't mind her," Griselda whispered. "She's mad because she hasn't attended the Union Ceremony yet. She's already fifteen!"

"Then why's she here?"

"Because her family sold her to the queen for money," Griselda whispered. "With the taxes going up, many families sell their children."

Hannah felt bile rise in her throat. "Have you attended the ceremony yet?"

"Oh my, yes! I was thirteen."

"You got married when you were thirteen?"

"Married? No, of course not." Griselda sounded horrified at the prospect. "I'll not marry. My job is scullery maid."

"If you aren't married, then what is the Union Ceremony?" Hannah asked.

"You know. That's why you're here, isn't it? How old are you?"

"I'm thirteen."

Griselda nodded. "And your moon phase?"

For a moment, Hannah was taken aback. Then she put two and two together. "That's none of your business!" she snapped.

"I beg your pardon," Griselda said. "It's not mine, but Her Majesty will find out. She always does."

Hannah felt icy fingers creep up her back. "The Union Ceremony is—"

"Of course it is," Griselda said. "Every one of us goes through it. It's a fact of life. Only then can we become adults."

"That's barbaric! Why don't you try to escape?"

"Shh!" Griselda hissed. "Someone'll hear you! Anyway, where would we go? Here we get good food and are taken care of. All who pledge allegiance to the queen are safe."

"Not like the Imperialites, eh, Gris?" Madeleine called.

"The who?" Hannah asked.

"Troublemakers," Madeleine said. "They spread false rumors about our queen."

Griselda cleared her throat nervously. "Now come. I must show you what to do."

She led Hannah toward the back of the scullery and stopped before a large wooden trough. "There is bread dough here. You must knead the dough for thirty minutes before each baking."

She handed Hannah a round instrument with a rotating handle and sharp, metal blade. "Her Majesty often likes cornbread as well. You must grind the kernels into a fine powder before they can be used. This process takes two hours." Hannah winced.

"To the right of the kneading trough is the butter churn. We'll bring both the corn and cream to you whenever they are needed."

Hannah's head was swimming with all the instructions, but Griselda was not finished. "Then, of course, you will be required to wash dishes. We'll bring you soap and water when it is time. Now you may start kneading the dough."

Hannah stood in front of the trough. Slowly she plunged her hands into the squishy mass and gasped. Her hands sank down into the cold mixture. The dough rose up to her elbows. "How much bread does the queen eat?" she cried.

"Her appetite is insatiable," Griselda said.

Steeling herself, Hannah began to heave the heavy, doughy mass from the trough. Before two minutes had passed, her arms were tingling with fatigue. She had a feeling it was going to be a long day.

brandon's task

Brandon sighed with contentment. Sitting at Marigold's plain wooden table, he swallowed the last mouthful of vegetable broth.

"Thanks so much, ma'am," he said. "The broth was delicious."

"I'm glad you're pleased, young Brandon," Marigold said in delight. "You're like my Jamal. Vegetable broth is his favorite as well."

Beside Brandon, a slender young man snorted. "He likes everything, Mother. He's a pig!"

"Mind your manners, Marshall," Marigold cried. "He's doing his job. There's no reason to resent him."

Brandon listened to the exchange between mother and son. He was unsure if Marshall was jealous of his brother or concerned for him.

On his left side, Mendel rose to his feet. "Thank ya for the pick-me-up, Marigold," he said quickly. "I suppose we'd better be gettin' back."

Marigold stood too. "Come on out to the bakeshop with us, Brandon," she said. "I must speak to you."

Brandon rose and followed them.

Marshall glared after the retreating boy but didn't say anything. He remained seated.

"It's so quiet back here now," Marigold murmured, "and the absence of smells! It's unbelievable!"

At the back of the hut, Marigold, Brandon, and Mendel entered the tiny building. Mendel had to duck to fit inside.

A wooden table crowded with various cooking utensils and bags of ingredients was the only furniture. "Jamal's talent for baking is unsurpassed in Crimlia," Marigold explained proudly. "It wasn't often we could obtain cream for éclairs, but whenever we could, they would melt in the mouth!"

"I've tried his bread," Brandon informed her. "There's something different about it that I can't explain."

"You do not have to explain to me. The difference is that he puts himself into his baking."

Brandon did not say anything. After a moment, Marigold spoke, "I am glad you did not spare me, but you told me the truth about where he is. I am not surprised."

"But why?" Brandon asked.

"Because his father instructed him to go to Salak's palace. He is always obedient. He and his father are of one mind and one spirit."

"Who is his father?"

"The Imperial Lord," Marigold said simply.

"But, I do not understand. How could—"

"Nothing is impossible for Him. My Moon Phase had just come upon me for the first time. I knew I would be taken by force to Salak's palace."

"For the Union Ceremony? You would be married to Joakim?"

"Ah! You know about Joakim, then?" For a moment, she blinked rapidly as if holding back tears, then she laughed bitterly. "Salak does not condone marriage. We Imperialites only marry in secret. No, lad. I was to be taken to the palace to be forced."

Brandon's stomach somersaulted. "She watches while this happens?"

"Yes, lad." It was Mendel who spoke. "Boys are taken when they are twelve, and girls are closely monitored to determine when the time is right."

"That's disgusting! Why can't she be stopped?"

"The time is drawing near when she will be," Marigold said. "When my Moon Phase came, an Eaglia, one of the Imperial Lord's messengers, came to me. He said I had been chosen to bear the Imperial Lord's son, but it was up to me to make the final decision."

"What was it like?"

"Beyond description. I was shrouded in brilliant light. It was like being enveloped by love itself. Soon, Salak's soldiers arrived to take me to the palace. You'd be surprised, but they're actually quite nice at first. I think even they do not like the task they must perform. During the ceremony, you are given a punch made from the juice of Aquaberries. The punch prevents pregnancy. I refused to drink, but Salak pried open my mouth and poured the liquid down my throat. Immediately, I became sick. She knew something was wrong."

"What happened?"

"She forced me to stand before a beautiful mirror, and it was as if she peered into my very soul! I was so frightened! Her livid face still haunts me to this day. She made me stay imprisoned in her dungeon, forcing me to drink awful-tasting potions, but they would not stay down. I remained there for a month receiving nourishment from Eaglias. They brought me broth and bread. After a month, the same Eaglia who'd delivered the message led me away from Salak's prison."

"And you and Joakim were married?"

"That's right. In my parents' house, in the dead of night."

Brandon's head was reeling. "People have to have babies eventually. What does the queen do?"

"Of course, she cannot prevent pregnancy all the time. Harem women are allowed two births; then they are forced to work in the palace all the rest of their lives. When a baby is born, Salak always knows. The babies in the palace harem are branded and trained to be her workers. Babies of Imperialite parents are taken by force and branded, but she is not allowed to keep them. The branding of those babies is pure spite on her part."

Anger filled Brandon's heart. "If the Imperial Lord is so powerful, why doesn't he destroy Salak?"

"People in Crimilia still desire her. You've seen for yourself the luxuries those who serve her receive. She promises them pleasure. She will not leave because people do not want her to. The Imperial Lord will force no one to love him if they choose not to."

"What about Jamal, Marshall, and Jordan? Did they attend the ceremony?"

Marigold smiled broadly. "No. Salak could not locate them. Praise His name!"

"What?"

Marigold nodded. "I hid them in this bakeshop. Joakim was also an excellent carpenter. Look."

She walked to a wooden plank situated on the ground. Stooping, she raised it and pointed. A gaping hole was visible.

"When Jamal was four, Joakim built this hideout. Jamal was always being harassed by Salak's soldiers when he played outside. Once, he was bitten by a snake! Joakim said if there was ever any trouble to use the passage under the plank. When the time came, I prayed that the boys would be protected, and the soldiers never discovered the hiding place. Jamal later told me that an Eaglia stood guard over them till the soldiers left. Only he and Jordan could see it. I think that's why Marshall—" Her smile wavered. Then, she said, "Other people have used the passage as well. I wish I could hide everyone, but doing so would cause her to try and destroy us all."

Brandon was silent for a moment. He considered all the things he'd learned about this strange land and its malevolent ruler. He thought of Jamal's kindness. At last, he said, "What can I do to help?"

Marigold surveyed him closely. "This mission is up to you, lad." Groping among the array of plain baking implements, she brought forth a glittering, jeweled bowl made of delicate porcelain. "Take this bowl to Jamal. An Eaglia brought it to me yesterday. She said, 'A boy with a leg brace will come to you. Entrust the bowl to him.'"

Brandon remembered the look of compassion in Jamal's eyes—a look that seemed to penetrate to his very soul. He thought of Jamal's banter with Jordan. "All right," he said. Reaching out a hand, he clasped the brilliant bowl with trembling fingers.

Marigold smiled. "Now, Mendel. Let's get you some bread for market day next week."

salak's souvenir

"You're taking a long time with that corn," Griselda observed.

Hannah, her hands bruised and swollen, slowly rotated the metal handle on the grinding machine. The sharp, steel blade screeched as it crushed corn kernels. So much corn! Hannah had burned her hands on the stones of the baking hearth. She'd cut her fingers while learning how to use the grinder. Her hands had splinters from the wooden handle of the butter churn. Three weeks had passed since she'd begun work in the scullery. Hannah despaired of ever being free.

At night, she'd fall into bed, her whole body aching from lifting masses of bread dough from the gigantic trough. Salak would come to her with lamb's broth and Trifles of Inertia. She would eat greedily and then fall into a heavy sleep.

During the day, Hannah's mind would be preoccupied with the endless work. At night, she would be so tired she could not think of anything but sleep.

"Will you be done soon?" Griselda demanded.

"I hope so," Hannah sighed.

"Well, hurry. Salak wants you to take a breakfast tray down to the dungeon."

Oh, no! Hannah had almost forgotten the strange man. Would Jamal still be there? Angrily, she rotated the handle of the grinder. Her head ached from the constant screeching.

At long last, she set the grinder aside. She stamped over to where Madeleine was loading plates onto a tray.

"Here," Madeleine snapped. "Hurry up! There's lots of dishes to wash."

Gasping at the weight of the tray, Hannah struggled through the herd of girls. Some stirred pots of fragrant sauces. Others chopped vegetables and prepared meats. After several days, she'd grown accustomed to the different smells and the constant activity. Queen Salak must have requested chicken for her lunch. The sharp odor of chicken fat filled the room.

Slowly, Hannah used her cane to locate the door to the dungeon. She couldn't imagine what Jamal had to eat today. The tray was much heavier than the last time. She did notice the familiar smell of oatmeal. To her surprise, Hannah felt her mouth water. How long had it been since she'd tasted oatmeal?

In the dungeon, the air was freezing cold. Hannah shivered. The *drip-drip* sound of water could be clearly heard. Besides this sound, the dungeon was silent.

She groped along the wall until she found the corner where she turned right. Her cane touched the doorjamb of Jamal's cell. Groping for the table, she placed the tray upon it.

"I've brought your breakfast," she murmured.

Movement within the cell was slower than before. She heard labored breathing. "Hello, Hannah," the familiar voice whispered. Hannah was startled at how weak and hoarse the voice sounded.

"Hello," she said. "I think you have oatmeal today." Why was she wasting her time talking to him?

"I see," he said. "I will not eat."

"But you sound so weak," Hannah protested. "Why not?"

"I am nourished by something more substantial, the communion with my Father," he said simply. "Besides, I will not give her the satisfaction."

Hannah hesitated. "Can I get you anything at all?"

"Some water would be nice," he said. His voice held the trace of a smile. "I see you have been working hard. Do you have time to think?"

Anger rose to the surface. "You're too nosy!" Hannah snapped. It unnerved her that this man always seemed to know what she was thinking.

Jamal laughed feebly. "You do not have to answer me. That water would hit the spot."

In spite of herself, Hannah smiled. "I'll be right back."

As the girl's footsteps faded away, Jamal leaned forward to peer at the loaded breakfast tray. Oatmeal, thick with milk and cinnamon, sat in a prideful place in the center surrounded by eggs, bacon, and sweet rolls. His stomach growled. "Salak?" he called. "Come out!"

A rustling sound preceded Salak's appearance. She'd changed from her serpent to her human form. Jamal peered into the hate-filled eyes. Salak looked away first. "Show me what you want me to see," he whispered.

Salak grinned. "Don't you want to eat first? I'm afraid this sight might put you off your food."

"For the past three weeks, you've brought dancing girls from the harem to perform for me. You've shown me my mother pining away in your hated looking glass. You forced Hannah to come before me again. Do what you came to do today."

Salak's nostrils flared. "I'll show you when I'm good and ready!" she snarled. "What I should do is force-feed you! Nothing would give me more pleasure than to see you vomit!" Pure, undiluted hatred shot from her eyes.

"You would force me to eat like you forced my mother to drink?"

Salak sucked in her breath. With a flourish, she brought from behind her back a silver platter with a cloth-covered object. "Herman and Hermia are wonderful tools," she gloated in triumph, "as is that sniveling Sally, Hermia's daughter. Behold, fool, the condition of those who defy me!" She ripped the cloth away. There, in grisly pride, sat Jordan's head.

Those upstairs in the scullery heard an earsplitting cry of pain. The cry pierced through to the very marrow of their bones. Hannah, who had been filling a cup with water, froze in shock.

Back in the dungeon, Salak's laughter rang out sharply. It was a terrifying sound—brittle and sharp like chips of ice. "Would a loving father allow such cruel treatment to occur?" she cried in exultation. "Renounce him, Jamal! Hate him!"

Jamal, his voice choked, managed to say, "It is written: 'Those who pursue truth will be persecuted. Happy are they.'"

"Persecuted?" Salak guffawed. "You'll be persecuted, all right. I salivate as I think of the day I shall have you at my mercy!"

Jamal did not respond. Suddenly, footsteps rushed down the stairs. "Go," he said to the queen. "You wouldn't want those who trust in you to see how you really are."

Salak had already changed into her serpent form. She slithered into the shadows as Hannah appeared with the water.

"Here," Hannah called. "Are you all right?"

Jamal took the cup of water she held out. "I will leave this place soon," he said.

Hannah nodded. "What did you do, anyway?"

"I came of my own free will. Tell me, Hannah, what do you enjoy doing?"

Hannah hesitated. Should she talk to this man? Finally, she said, "I love to play music. I played the flute in the band at my old school, but I don't take lessons anymore."

Jamal nodded. "I know. You're talented. I love music as well. In my bakeshop, I always sang as I worked."

"Do you bake a lot?"

"Yes. I bake pastries. I have a sweet tooth." His eyes twinkled, and Hannah heard a hint of a smile in his voice. "I also bake the Bread of Freedom."

"What?" Hannah asked.

"The Bread of Freedom. Anyone who partakes will live forever."

Hannah frowned. "I better get back to the scullery. I have to wash dishes."

"Yes," Jamal said. "I understand. Thank you for the water."

Hannah turned and began to walk away. "Hannah?" Jamal called.

She turned around. "Brandon is well."

Hannah shivered. She walked away into the darkness.

In the cell, Jamal put the cup of water to his lips. Instantly, the clear liquid reeked. He tasted vinegar on his tongue. Laughter filled the air. "See you tomorrow, Jamal," Salak's voice hissed.

Jamal sighed. *How much longer, Father?* he thought desperately.

Then, he reached into the pocket of his robe. He withdrew a piece of cherry wood and a carving knife.

Images of Jordan filled his brain—the boisterous little boy, the teenager who loved spending time outdoors.

"He's safe now," his Father's voice whispered. It too was filled with anguish.

"I know, but I'll miss him here." With tears flowing unchecked from his eyes, he set to work with the wood and carving knife.

ambush

"Are you sure you're ready for this, lad?" Mendel's voice had lost its harshness. Over the past three weeks, he'd grown increasingly fond of the visitor at his home.

Brandon looked up from where he was piling vegetables into bags. "Yes, I'm positive. I've been to the market with you and seen those kids. Jamal's bread changes them from scared and sad to happy. He is doing a good work."

"Yes, lad, he is," Ursula called. She was wrapping up some food for Brandon to take with him. "I'm afraid it's the usual. What I wouldn't give for some cheese! I've almost forgotten what it tastes like."

Brandon nodded. "Or some cheese pizza with pepperoni!"

"I'll never understand ya, boy!" Ursula laughed. She handed Brandon the paper-wrapped bundle of bread and apples.

"Thanks for being so kind to me," Brandon said. "I've loved spending time with you."

"Don't mention it," Mendel said gruffly. "Here. I'll take ya as far as Nunmal. The palace is two more towns from there."

"Will Marigold be all right?"

"Why, of course. She's gone to stay with Eliza for a while to comfort her. Marigold's been persecuted by that hussy queen since the day she turned thirteen! She's had to be stronger than anybody I know."

"I still can't believe it!" Ursula exclaimed angrily. "Whatever will become of us? Now we make children do our dirty work!"

Brandon thought about the last time he and Mendel had visited Marigold. She'd come out of the hut, her eyes swollen and barely able to walk. A message written in scarlet letters on heavy parchment had come from the palace:

> My dear Marigold,
>
> I regret to inform you of the death of your nephew, Jordan Ernest. He was executed yesterday at the bidding of King Herman. I received the word from Gretchen Smithe, scullery maid at King Herman's palace. I thought it best to inform you of this news before you heard it from some unscrupulous source. My prayers go out to you.

The letter had been unsigned, but Marigold had seemed to know who the sender was. She'd found out that Hermia had prompted her own eleven-year-old daughter, Sally, to ask for the head of Jordan after she'd sung for a drunken King Herman at his birthday celebration. Of course, Hermia had been prompted to do this by Salak.

"How did you find this out?" Brandon had asked.

Marigold's face clouded. "From this. It arrived a day after the anonymous letter came." Going over to a table, she'd taken a piece of parchment into her hands.

On the parchment, a picture of a young girl holding a blood-drenched head on a platter had been sketched in garish shades of brown, pink, and red. Underneath the picture, musical notes had been drawn, and a crude message had been scrawled: "I hear Sally is having nightmares now. What do you think? Can the Imperial Lord really be as loving as you claim? Give my regards to Eliza!"

Brandon had felt lightheaded and nauseous. If anything, this childish taunting by Queen Salak made him even more determined to find Jamal.

He and Mendel left the hut. Ursula waved until they'd faded from view. They took turns pulling the cart, and the journey was a silent one.

Brandon clutched the beautiful bowl that Marigold had given him. He still wondered what was so special about a porcelain bowl. He simply could not imagine.

On the outskirts of Nunmal, Mendel stopped the cart. "I'll be praying for you, Brandon," he said.

"Thanks again," Brandon said.

"Here's something to help you." Mendel took some parchment from his pocket. On the parchment, a crude map was drawn. "You follow this map, and it'll lead ya right to the palace. You're sure you don't want me to go with you?"

"Don't be silly, Mendel," Brandon said. "You can't abandon Ursula."

Mendel nodded. "You're right there, lad."

Suddenly, without warning, he reached out and gave Brandon a hug. Brandon blushed.

"Thanks," he murmured. Clutching the bowl, map, and food, he set out on his journey.

Brandon was surprised that he didn't feel as tired as when he'd first arrived in Crimilia. The three weeks working with Mendel in the vegetable garden had strengthened him more than he realized.

The air smelled strongly of honeysuckle. A light breeze played with Brandon's hair.

Studying the map carefully, Brandon walked slowly along the dirt roads.

"There he is! Grab him!" several harsh voices cried at once.

Brandon had only just a moment to wonder who the voices were talking about, when he was jerked savagely from behind. Figures appeared from nowhere. They lunged and pummeled his back and sides. "Hand it over! In the name of Her Majesty, Queen Lucinda, Empress of Crimilia!"

Hands poked and prodded him. One hand snatched his leg that was encased in the brace, and he crumpled to the ground. Brandon bellowed in pain.

"Here it is, Armand!" a deep voice rumbled. "I've found it!"

"Good! What about him, then?"

"She didn't say. Take him with us?"

From in the distance, Brandon, his mind whirling, could barely make out two approaching figures. "No!" the deep voice said, "we'll leave him here as an example. She just wanted the bowl!"

Without warning, several pairs of boots and large fists kicked and gouged Brandon's flesh. He screamed and tried to fight. His bad leg was wrenched so badly he was scared it had been dislocated.

There was a flurry of movement out of the corner of his eye, a sound of clashing metal, and an ear-splitting scream. Then, a boot slammed into Brandon's forehead, and he knew no more.

the gift

Hannah tiptoed stealthily down the dungeon stairs. Her progress was much quicker now that she was not carrying a tray. It was late afternoon, and she felt some strange feeling surge within her.

Hannah's heart was pounding. A week had passed since the second time she'd brought breakfast to Jamal. For some unexplained reason, she'd felt compelled to check on him.

I must be going crazy, she thought in disgust.

The drudgery in the scullery continued day after day. Hannah knew that if she ever got home again, she'd never want another slice of cornbread!

Her thoughts made her stop short. If she would get home! She had to!

Starting to walk again, she found the corner where she turned to the right. She reached Jamal's cell.

"Hello," she called.

"Hello, Hannah." This time, the voice was barely audible. Hannah felt fear grip her insides like a vise.

"What's wrong?" she asked harshly.

"I am just tired, that is all," Jamal murmured. "You are looking stronger than before. Are you well?"

"I'm all right. Do you want anything?"

"No, but thank you. The time is drawing near for me to go."

"Go? Go where?"

"Different places in Crimilia. Tell me, do you have time to think now?"

Hannah hesitated. "I'm quite busy," she admitted. "I have a lot to do in the scullery."

"What about at night?"

"I do all right!" Hannah snapped. "Have you always been so nosy?"

Jamal laughed. "Yes," he admitted, "I like to get to know people. For instance, I have a feeling you shouldn't be here. Your coming proves you're sneaky."

Hannah blushed. "Yeah," she admitted, "a little."

"Well, it was kind of you to come." His voice was fading more and more. "I must sleep, now, but before I do, I have something to give you."

Hannah felt her cheeks grow red. "What do you mean?"

Without saying a word, Jamal passed an object through the crack under the door. Hannah heard the sound of wood hitting the dungeon floor and bent down. She groped until she discovered a thin, smooth instrument of some sort. She picked it up and explored it with her fingers.

The instrument was pear-shaped and made of smooth wood that had holes carved into its body. A rectangular mouthpiece was carved into the top.

"Thanks," she managed to say. "What is it?"

"It's a longolia. You play it like you would a flute."

"You mean to say you carve things, and you didn't make a key to get you out of here?" Hannah said incredulously.

"I told you I chose to come here. Try to play the longolia. I want to make sure it works."

Tentatively, Hannah placed the instrument to her lips. She blew softly, and the sweetest note she'd ever heard issued forth. She stopped playing and just stood, dumbfounded.

"Do you know any songs?" Jamal asked.

"Y-Yeah," Hannah stammered. Slowly, she began to play "From This Moment," one of her favorites. The longolia's music soared around the dungeon, light and sweeter than birdsong.

After that song was finished, Jamal clapped in appreciation, but Hannah did not hear him. She had launched into "Wade into the Water," a song the elementary school band had played in a concert a year before the accident. As she played, her spirits felt lighter than they had in days.

"Well done!" Jamal said happily. A little strength had returned to his voice.

"Th-Thank you," Hannah managed to say, "But why—"

"It helped pass the time, and it will help you to have something other than scullery work to think about. By the way, have you had any more Trifles of Inertia?"

Hannah jumped. No. She hadn't had any in over a week. Salak had stopped coming to her. Hannah remembered how she often lay awake at night, longing for the rich, satisfying sweets.

Now, strangely, she didn't think of them with as much longing as before. She shook her head.

"I better be getting back to work. I just wanted to see how you were," she said.

"Thank you, Hannah. The gift of your visit fills me with joy! I will leave here soon. If you want to come with me, I'll come to your chamber to collect you."

Hannah didn't say anything. After a moment, she turned away. Then she turned back. "Thanks again for the, the longolia. It's beautiful!" Then, without another word, she walked away.

Jamal sank back onto the floor. "Thank you, Father," he whispered.

the bowl of abundance

"You've got it?" Salak barked.

"Yes, Your Majesty," Aufeld said.

"Give it to me!"

Aufeld held out the beautiful porcelain bowl. It glittered among all the jewels in the throne room, shining with a brilliance that far surpassed the finery that surrounded it.

Salak's lips curled into a smile terrifying to behold. "Excellent," she hissed. "Well done." She ran a crimson hand through her flowing hair. "You will be rewarded," she smiled again. "And the boy?"

"He has been beaten beyond recognition."

Salak laughed. "You may leave me now."

Aufeld fidgeted nervously. "Um, my queen…"

"Well? What is it?"

"Armand—"

"Yes? What about him?"

"He is dead, Your Majesty. Some Imperialite zealots—"

"Is he?" Salak asked. Her voice was so composed that Aufeld's mouth opened in astonishment. "Leave me, Aufeld. I'll send for you later so you can claim your reward."

Aufeld eyed the queen with open anticipation. Then he left the room.

Shaking with mirth, Salak leaned back into the plush cushions of her throne. She held the bowl in front of her, admiring its every angle.

"It's mine," she whispered gleefully. "All mine."

Then she turned to her mirror. After admiring her own reflection for five minutes, she rotated the glass. "Show me Jamal," she intoned.

The glass darkened. Salak waited. No picture appeared. What was going on?

"Show me!" Salak snarled. "I want to see him!"

Still the mirror remained clouded. Salak rose angrily and stormed from the room. She clutched the bowl in her hands.

At Jamal's cell, she stopped and glared inside. "Hiding from me was not part of the bargain!" she raged.

"I did not hide from you. Your own pride blinded you. You can't see anything that does not benefit your plans."

"Spare me the lecture!" she hissed. "Something has been going on! What is it?"

Jamal smiled. "You speak of hiding things. Don't you have something to show me?"

Salak frowned. Then she laughed. "Very well. Now's as good a time as any."

With a flourish, she held out the porcelain bowl. Her eyes gleamed with triumph. "Observe, your Lordship."

Before Jamal's eyes, streams of gold coins appeared out of thin air and cascaded into the beautiful bowl. The bowl grew so full of coins that even Salak staggered under its weight. Finally, she snapped her fingers and the flow of money stopped. Jamal saw that the bowl was still only halfway full.

"See, Jamal? The Bowl of Abundance! Anything you desire will appear. Do you know what this means?"

She snapped her fingers again. Instantly, a breathtaking sight materialized. Women, men, and children flocked to Jamal's side. They held out their hands imploringly as if seeking assistance. Salak gestured to the bowl.

"Look. With this money, you will have access to every kingdom in Crimlia! You can help all the people you want! People will cater to your every need. I know. People come to me all the time. Men come for pleasure. I can bring women to you. You'll want for nothing."

Salak's breathing was labored with excitement. Jamal too was breathing hard. She could see that his heart was pounding. "All this will be yours," she whispered, "if you will only open your heart to me. Come. Bow down to me and have riches beyond your wildest imagination! Why must you always do things your father's way? Break free of his tyranny as I did!"

For a moment Jamal hesitated.

"Partake of what I offer and be free." Her voice was softer than the cooing of a dove.

Jamal's hand stretched toward the bowl. Every fiber of his being ached for the power that was offered him.

Then, his head suddenly rose up. "Begone, Salak! It is written: 'Worship only the Imperial Lord! Serve him exclusively!'"

Surprisingly, Salak was not perturbed. "You're strong, Jamal," she whispered, "but I'll see you again very soon. Enjoy your freedom because it will be short-lived." Softly, she began to sing a strange, dark dirge. The melody was in a minor key and was quite startling to hear when sung by such an astonishingly beautiful voice. The Bowl of Abundance rose from Salak's hands, and Jamal watched as it was encased in a cocoon-like web of transparent filaments. "Reach for it," the queen ordered. Jamal turned away from her, but she grabbed his wrists and brutally crushed his hands against the cocoon. Jamal screamed as red burns erupted onto his wrists and hands. "Even you cannot retrieve my prize," Salak mocked. She savagely released him and looked for a long moment at his face. She laughed and turned to go.

As she turned away, a deafening flurry of wings resounded. Startled, she turned back.

Jamal lay crumpled on the cell floor. He was shaking with fatigue and pain. Five Eaglias, brilliant to behold, hovered around him. They gently lifted him to a sitting position. Salak bit her lip in disbelief as she watched one of them rub a fragrant ointment into his hands and wrists.

"Well done, my Lord!" One of the Eaglias was saying. Others were handing Jamal meat, bread, broth, and cakes. "Eat and be strengthened," the Eaglias chorused.

A fleeting memory of Salak's own service as an Eaglia invaded her mind. A feeling for which she no longer had words stabbed through her like a knife. Blinking rapidly, she turned from the hated sight and fled.

surprising happenings

"I think he's comin' 'round now," a gravelly voice rumbled.

Brandon's head was throbbing. He tasted blood in his mouth.

Groaning, he sat up slowly. His head began to spin crazily.

"It's all right," the gruff voice intoned. "You'd best lie down now. You've got a nasty bump on your head."

"W-Where am I?" Brandon croaked.

"In me home, lad. There's no cause for worry. They're gone now."

"Who's gone?"

"Those good-for-nothing followers of Salak! I'd've killed all of 'em if I'd had a chance!"

Despite his pounding head, Brandon sat up again. "You killed someone?"

"Aye. He's not the first one I've finished off! Now lie back. Lydia's gettin' you some broth."

Brandon obeyed. "You're askin' for trouble for us all, Samenal," a second male voice said. "She might send someone here any moment."

"Hope she does, Barson!" Samenal said defiantly. "I'd kill her in a minute!"

A thin woman tiptoed into the room. "He's awake, I see," she said.

"Yes, m'dear," Samenal said.

"Hello, lad. Glad to see you're in the land of the livin'," Lydia said cheerfully. "Here's some vegetable broth. Sorry it's all we have."

Turning to Samenal, she said, "We're runnin' low. Is Marigold expected tomorrow?"

"Aye."

Samenal helped prop a cushion behind Brandon's back. Brandon sipped the broth appreciatively and looked around the small room. The major difference in this hut was that knives were arranged in stone cases along the walls. Intricately carved statues stood upon workbenches and tables. "How long have I been here?" he finally asked.

"Four days," Lydia said.

Brandon gazed at the three adults. Lydia was petite and had a kind face. However, her shoulder-length chestnut hair was flecked with gray. Samenal, the man who'd helped Brandon sit up, was muscular, and his face was etched with worry lines. Barson was short and balding. His eyes constantly darted around the room.

"What's your name, lad?" Samenal asked.

"Brandon."

"Well, Brandon, you're in Nunmal. You'll be all right."

Brandon's jumbled mind was slowly returning to normal. He remembered the struggle with the bandits. Grenades of pain exploded in his bad leg. "I can't take much more of this," he mumbled.

"Nor can we, lad," Samenal said. "Pray the Deliverer will come soon!"

"He's here already," Brandon blurted.

Samenal smiled indulgently. "And whom do you mean, lad?"

"The baker, Jamal."

After a moment, Lydia gasped, and Barson fidgeted nervously. Samenal glared.

"Wherever did ya get such a notion, lad?" he barked.

"I saw him, and I've tasted his bread. Not only that, but I've gotten to know his mother. Ursula Maloney told me that he heals people, too."

"Ya say a lot, lad. He doesn't heal everybody." Samenal's voice was sharp with bitterness. "You should know." He pointed to Brandon's brace.

"Samenal, hold your tongue!" Barson snarled.

"I only say what's true! What about Priscilla? Andrew? Dan?"

"Sam," Lydia said gently, "he was only five then."

"The Deliverer heals everyone. Anyway, why would a deliverer come in the form of a baker? We need someone who'll gather together an army!"

Brandon looked around the hut once more. The collection of knives and the statues told their own story. Samenal must be a woodcarver. Apparently, something had happened to people in his family that he thought Jamal could have prevented. Had he abandoned his woodcarving career to pursue vengeance? Sympathy for the man invaded Brandon's heart, and he couldn't help but think about his own life. He thought about the accident that had robbed him of his own identity and about the anger that he tried so hard to hide from others.

Now, he looked closely into Samenal's eyes. "I don't know everything about Jamal," he admitted. "I just know he'll free you all."

"You all?" Lydia inquired. "What about you?"

Brandon blushed. "I was supposed to help him, and I failed."

A small smile returned to Samenal's lips. "Don't worry about that part of it, lad. I'll get it back."

Lydia glared at her husband. "You're not goin' to that palace! Especially not to pick up a blasted bowl!"

"It's the principle of the thing, m'dear! Those barbarians have gotta be taught a lesson!"

Brandon's head began to reel again. He lay back down and listened to the low talking around him. Soon he drifted off into a deep sleep.

Before the dawn broke, Brandon was awake. The vegetable broth had invigorated him, and he felt ready to look for Jamal.

Slowly he heaved himself to his feet. On a small table, he discovered the crude map that Mendel had drawn. His bad leg still cramped, but he gritted his teeth and tiptoed from the house. He would not allow someone to steal and risk being killed because of his mistake. The only thing he could think to do was find Jamal.

Outside, the air was heavy and pressed down on Brandon's head. He was aware that everything was quiet.

By the middle of the morning, Brandon's leg was aching. He found an oak tree and sat beneath it.

After a few moments, he felt ready to move along.

After another half hour of walking, Brandon looked closely at the map. He saw that Mendel had included a sketch of Trimland Hill and Marigold's hut.

If I go there, maybe she can tell me if he's still at the palace.

Marigold's hut looked the same, but the atmosphere was different. There was a festive feeling in the air. Brandon was surprised by the change.

As he drew nearer to the hut, his nostrils were assailed by a delicious fragrance—vanilla, sugar, and eggs—the kind of smell he remembered from his grandmother's house when she baked birthday cakes!

Excitement filled Brandon's soul. He felt like running but decided against it.

Suddenly, he heard a joyful cry. "Brandon!"

Brandon fell into Marigold's arms. "Thank the Imperial Lord you're safe! I was beside myself!"

"This place seems different," Brandon said.

Marigold's smile broadened. "It is! Jamal is home for a day or two! I returned home yesterday from Eliza's, and he arrived this morning!"

Brandon's heart leaped. He followed Marigold into the bakery. The delicious smells grew stronger.

"Jamal! He's come!" Marigold beamed.

Jamal straightened up from the hearth where he had been watching a cake pan. His face was tired, but his smile was broad, and happiness poured from him like a fountain of water.

"It's great to see you again, Brandon!"

Brandon smiled sheepishly. "I'm afraid I—"

Jamal nodded, and his smile did not fade. "It wasn't your fault. Everything will work out." For a moment, his smile wavered. Then he gestured toward the hearth. "How does the cake look, Mother?"

Marigold beamed. "Fit for a princess! Although," her eyes twinkled, "I'm not sure Prissy Patricia would agree with me!" Mother and son burst out laughing.

"Prissy Patricia?" Brandon asked in bewilderment.

"Ah, yes! Her father used to work as chief tailor in the palace," Marigold explained. "He's left Salak's service now, but Patricia's used to the finer things in life. Don't worry, though. She has a good heart."

"This is her wedding cake," Jamal explained. "Her wedding's tonight in the town of Camrill, just on the outskirts of Nunmal. She'll be married in her father's home. You're welcome to come."

Marigold nodded. "Please do, Brandon. We'd love to have you."

"Sure," Brandon said. "Thanks."

Patricia's father's house was a hut identical to all the others Brandon had seen. Despite the close quarters, a large crowd had gathered. Brandon noticed that the majority of the party-goers were simply dressed. However, he saw a few men who were dressed in expensive-looking robes. Their heads were held high as they swept by the humbler-looking groups. Brandon didn't know why, but he felt uncomfortable around them.

"Marigold? Who are those people?" he asked.

She frowned slightly. "They're the Overseers of the Imperialites. It's rumored that they serve Salak in secret."

The wedding guests chatted and gestured toward a table with a modest but delicious-looking meal upon it. In the center of the table in the place of honor was Jamal's wedding cake.

The wedding itself was more interesting than any that Brandon had ever attended. During the ceremony, the bride and groom drank wine from the same cup. They also performed an intricate dance; their legs bound together with twine. They had to dance in perfect harmony, or they would fall.

After the wedding ceremony, the reception began. Music was played by a small band of musicians, and the people danced joyfully. Brandon noticed that Jamal was an excellent dancer. The baker danced, laughed heartily, and ate food with relish. Jamal seemed to be having more fun than anyone else. At one point, he left the party, but he soon returned.

In the midst of the reception, Brandon noticed frenzied whispering going on between Patricia's father and some friends. "What shall we do? I don't have any more."

"Couldn't you use something else instead?"

Patricia's father snorted. "Of course not! It's traditional! What can we do?"

Brandon noticed Marigold making her way toward the group. "What is wrong, Horace?" she asked. "Can I help?"

"Not unless you have a cow to loan me! Rachel's not producing milk, and I'm out!"

Marigold looked concerned. "Wait a moment, Horace. I'll be right back."

Seething with curiosity, Brandon followed Marigold to the refreshment table. Jamal was handing a young woman a cup of wine. The woman wore a revealing gown, and waist-length blonde hair billowed around her.

Marigold touched Jamal on the shoulder and he turned. "Jamal, they have no milk. Rachel is not producing any more."

"Mother, this is Angela. She was outside, and I invited her in."

Marigold noticed the woman for the first time. Her cheeks grew red, but she extended her hand.

"Welcome," she said warmly. "There's plenty of food and drink. Please help yourself."

Angela turned a shocked face onto the older woman. "Are you mocking me?" she snapped.

Jamal touched Angela's hand. "No. You are here as my guest. Eat your fill." He turned back to his mother. "About the milk. Why do you come to me? The time has not yet arrived."

Marigold nodded. Then she turned away. "Brandon?" she whispered. "If he calls for you, please do whatever he asks." Then she walked away.

Brandon turned to follow her when a large man with a square jaw pushed past him and stamped toward the refreshment table. He wore one of the expensive-looking robes.

The man looked past Jamal, who was handing a slice of wedding cake to a little girl, to Angela, who was eating a slice of bread and cheese.

"Who let you in here?" he thundered.

Angela pointed at Jamal. Then she winked at the large man and continued eating the bread.

"You're not welcome here!" the man snarled. "This is a wedding, a pure ceremony. You're contaminating Horace's house!"

A large crowd of celebrators began to surge around the table. The room had gone deathly silent. Even the musicians were no longer playing.

"Mind your own business!" Brandon blurted before he could stop himself.

The man spun around and glared at the speaker. "Who are you?" he snapped. "Show some respect to your elders, boy! Anyway, you don't belong here, either!"

Jamal's voice, sharp and authoritative, cut through the gasps of the crowd. "Parker, both Brandon and Angela are my guests. They have every right to be here."

Parker glared. "You're an upstart, baker! These intruders were not issued invitations! Besides, the woman is a—"

"They were. By myself."

"What's all this?" The resonant voice of Horace filled the room. "Come, guests! Dance! Eat! Drink! It's a party!"

The crowd quickly dispersed. Parker glared venomously at Jamal, smiled weakly at Horace, then slid back into the crowd.

"Almost time for the Fertility Rite, folks!" Horace called. As he passed Brandon, the boy noticed a worried frown crease the father's brow.

"Brandon?" Jamal called.

Brandon trudged toward the refreshment table. "What is it?" he asked.

Jamal gestured to the corner of the room. "Please fill those five water jars over there. The well is out in the back."

Brandon nodded. He shuffled to the corner and lifted an earthenware jar. The jar was heavy and wide-brimmed. "I'll have to make several trips," Brandon called.

Jamal nodded, and Brandon trudged outside.

Slowly he tiptoed to the well and attached the rope to the neck of the jar. Thank goodness he had practice doing this at Mendel's!

The rope went slack, and Brandon pulled the jar to the surface. It was filled with water and was very heavy.

He staggered back toward Horace's dwelling.

"That young, impertinent freak!" a voice rang out in the darkness. Brandon nearly dropped the jar. "Who does he think he is?"

"Be patient, my friend," a gentler, male voice crooned. "You lash out too hastily."

"Annis, it's unbearable! I've known that insufferable baker for years. He's always contradicting me! I'm an official in the Imperial Lord's service! I deserve respect! That woman," he spat out the word with contempt, "does not belong here."

"As I say, patience. He won't be popular long. These people come and go. People will lose interest in him."

Parker grunted.

Brandon hurried as fast as he could back inside. He filled the other jars and carried them one by one to Jamal.

"Jamal! Two men outside—"

Jamal nodded but showed no concern. "Please take some water to Horace and have him taste it." He handed Brandon a cup filled to the brim.

Brandon was totally dumbfounded, but he shrugged.

Horace was talking in a hushed voice to some friends. Brandon approached him nervously. "Uh, sir?"

"Yes? Yes? What is it, boy?" Horace asked impatiently.

"Uh, Jamal wanted you to taste this."

Horace took the cup. "Water? What on earth for?"

Brandon shrugged.

Horace put the cup to his lips. Before he took a drink, Brandon saw the clear water turn yellow. He gasped.

Horace sipped from the cup. He sputtered and nearly dropped it. "What is—" he gulped.

Brandon saw that the water had turned into milk, and not just any milk. The milk was thick, and yellow cream floated on top. Brandon thought about cow's milk on Grandpa Nick's farm. The thicker the cream, the richer and more delicious the milk! His mouth began to water. The contrast between this milk and the substance used to murder Abigail was startling. If Brandon had needed proof of the more powerful person in the conflict between Salak and Jamal, then he'd just received it.

"What's going on?" Horace squeaked.

Horace's friends stared at him in fascination. "I guess the problem is solved," one of them said.

Horace grinned. "I suppose so. Well! What're we waiting for?"

He clapped his hands. "The Fertility Rite will begin! Everyone, join me in drinking a toast of milk to my lovely daughter, Patricia! Milk represents production and fertility. May the Imperial Lord open her womb, and may she and her husband live a long and prosperous life! May we all see better days in the future when the bonds of tyranny are broken!"

All the crowd gathered at the refreshment table. They helped themselves to cups of rich, pure milk.

Brandon tentatively sipped from his cup. His eyes opened in fascination. The milk was cold and sweet. He'd never tasted anything so creamy and refreshing.

"So, Horace," a guest called jovially. "You've been holding out on us! Where does that cow of yours graze? I've never tasted anything like this!"

Horace smiled. "The Imperial Lord has blessed us all!" he cried.

Brandon scanned the crowd for Jamal, but he was nowhere to be seen.

Outside, Jamal and Angela stood. Angela's face was flushed. She held out a hand and gently caressed Jamal's cheek.

"What can I offer you in return for your hospitality?" she whispered. "My services will be free, of course."

Jamal shook his head. "Nothing. I only give you the option of leaving Salak's service. Come and follow me."

Angela looked surprised. Then, without another word, she walked away.

Jamal stared after her for a moment. Then he turned and walked back into the celebration. Behind his back, a scarlet serpent slithered away into the darkness.

betrayal

"What is it that you wish to tell me?"

The throne room was bathed in translucent sunlight. A figure knelt before the queen's feet.

"I think she went to see him a few days before he left, Your Majesty. She was gone from the scullery for several minutes."

"How does she appear to you, now?" Salak's voice was sharp.

"She seems happier and not as tired. I think he gave her something—"

"Don't think anything, fool! Just report the facts!"

The figure trembled. "Forgive me."

Salak's voice softened. "You did right to come here. I hadn't anticipated…" Her voice trailed away. "Send Aufeld here!"

The figure rose to withdraw, but the queen raised a hand. "Wait."

Reaching into the pocket of her silk dress, she brought forth a metal tool with a sharp, pointed edge. Slowly, she began to chip away some of the gems that studded the frame of her Mirror of Revelation.

When she'd chiseled away twenty gems, she handed them to the figure. "Grind them into slivers and place them into the fermenting dough. They need ample time to be absorbed. The Day is drawing near."

The queen then handed the figure a bulging pouch of coins. "Well done. You may go to market tomorrow. Now, leave me!"

When the throne room door closed, the queen cursed in frustration. "She's mine! Leave her to me!"

Snatching her mirror, she located Hannah, who was polishing goblets. Salak's nostrils flared in fury. The girl did look happier! Well, she'd soon remedy that!

Plenty Palace was filled with the hurried sounds of scurrying feet and shouts. Hannah, who was washing dishes, felt an unexplained dread invade her mind.

Hannah did not know why, but she felt abandoned and lost. The days stretched ahead of her in a never-ending stream. Every time she tried to search for a way out of the palace, a scullery worker would discover her.

One morning a month earlier, she'd heard Griselda telling Madeleine that the prisoner in the dungeon had escaped. Hannah had remembered that the night before, Salak had come to her with Trifles of Inertia. A voice within her seemed to implore her to resist the sweets, but Hannah had been unable to do so. She'd slept for what seemed like hours, and then awakened to the news of Jamal's escape.

Hannah's hands were bruised beyond recognition. Her arms constantly ached from kneading troughs of heavy, unyielding bread dough. Her back and feet ached, and she had begun crying herself to sleep at night.

Despite all this, she constantly sought opportunities to play the longolia that Jamal had given her. She'd remembered many solos she'd played in the school band, and she'd even memorized some of the songs the scullery workers sang. Griselda was particularly fond of singing, and Hannah had begun joining in. The singing made the work go faster. Of course, when the queen was nearby, they never sang. Singing was forbidden.

Comfort flowed into every part of Hannah's body when she placed the wooden instrument to her lips. The longolia played notes of such purity that Hannah felt strength surge within her.

Queen Salak had not come to Hannah since that night a month ago. Hannah did not know what to think of this. Often a longing for the sweet trifles came over her in an intoxicating wave. At those times it was all she could do to focus on her work. However, when she played the longolia, the desire for the sweets dissipated.

"Hannah?" Griselda's voice rang out. "Her Majesty wishes to see you."

Hannah jumped and nearly dropped a crystal goblet. Swallowing hard, she turned to face Griselda. "Why?"

"I don't know, do I?" Griselda's voice was sharp. "She just asked for you."

Hannah placed the goblet on a shelf. "All right," she sighed.

"I'll take you to the throne room," Griselda said.

Hannah took her cane and followed Griselda down the twisting hallways. The birds in their cages continued to sing piteously.

Without warning, Griselda grasped Hannah's arm and pushed her into an alcove beside a cage. "No matter what she does to you, don't give her the longolia!" she whispered fiercely.

Hannah opened her mouth in amazement. "How do you—"

"I just know!" Griselda said impatiently. "I think someone else knows too. You must keep that instrument! It's your only weapon! I'll see what I can do, but you must reveal nothing to her. Do you understand?"

Hannah nodded. Then, she followed Griselda to the throne room.

Griselda opened the door and ushered Hannah inside.

"Ah! My newest scullery maid! Welcome!" Salak seemed delighted to see her. Hannah's nervousness began to ebb.

"Come forward, Hannah," the queen instructed.

Hannah approached the sound of the musical voice. She started to bow, but Salak detained her.

"No need for formalities. Sit down in this chair. Griselda, you may go."

Griselda hesitated, but then she withdrew. In the hallway, she breathed a quick prayer. Then she bolted toward Hannah's bedchamber. This spying business really frayed the nerves!

In the throne room, Hannah hesitantly sat down.

"I apologize for not coming to see you in so long, but I have been busy with affairs of state. Is your work going well?"

Hannah nodded. "I'm just tired," she admitted.

"That's understandable. Soon the work will be routine. Now, would you like something while we talk?"

Hannah's mouth began to water like mad. She knew what the "something" was.

Salak smiled knowingly. "Of course you would like them," she whispered. "Here." She placed a single piece of candy into Hannah's hand.

Hannah popped the sweet into her mouth. Dark chocolate, marshmallows, and vanilla custard exploded onto her tongue in an indescribable flavor. Hannah gasped in wonder.

"Is it good?" Salak's voice held a broad smile.

Hannah didn't bother answering. She was too overcome with the rich taste to speak. She felt giddy.

"You make exquisite bread," Salak said, "and you're not a slacker. I am proud to have you in my service."

Hannah felt herself blushing because of the praise. She longed for another trifle, preferably a whole box.

"Would you like some more?" Salak asked.

"Yes! Yes, please!" Hannah blurted. She realized she sounded like a childish idiot, but she couldn't stop herself. "It's been so long!"

"Yes, of course. You may have all you want, after you give me your longolia!"

The final words hit Hannah like a slap. Her ears rang, and she felt confused. "L-longolia?" she stammered.

"Yes, you fool! You went to see Jamal without my knowing, didn't you?" Salak's voice was icy. Hannah shivered. She knew that lying would be useless.

"I was just—he seemed so—"

"Seemed is the correct word! He seeks to destroy you. I am trying to help you. If you give me the longolia, you'll be safe from his influence!"

Hannah swallowed. "I won't!" she managed to say.

A stinging blow on her left cheek made Hannah's head spin. She tried to stand but felt Salak's hard hand slam into her other cheek.

"You're mine! You'll do as I say!" the queen hissed. "It's not in your room! Where is it?"

Hannah's head was throbbing, and her ears were ringing. She knew very well that the longolia was in her room. It was hidden under some underclothing. Why couldn't the queen find it?

"Where is it?" Salak's voice had lost all its composure. She was screaming now.

Suddenly, courage surged into Hannah's heart. "You'll never find it!" she cried defiantly.

"Very well," Salak's voice was smooth as silk. "We'll see how long you dare to defy me!" Her hand shot forward, and she hauled Hannah to her feet. "Stand over here, you wretched fool!"

She jerked the helpless girl toward her mirror and positioned her in front of it. She stared with bloodshot eyes into Hannah's mind.

Hannah tried to run but found that her feet would not budge. Salak grabbed Hannah's cane and flung it into a corner of the room.

"You've reached your Moon Phase!" she chortled. "This will be easier than I thought! Aufeld!"

As if on cue, the throne room door opened with a boom. Reverberating footsteps echoed. "Your Majesty?"

"This girl has reached her Moon Phase." The words hung like poison in the air. "The Union Ceremony is tomorrow night, but I think we need not wait till then, do you?"

All dignity forgotten, Hannah began to scream.

"Your Majesty?" Aufeld was saying. "I"

"Do it, slave!"

"But she's—"

Salak turned to the trapped girl. "Come, Aufeld. You serve me. Do as I say."

Hannah felt masculine hands grip her shoulders. Above her own pounding heart, she heard shrill laughter.

Above the maniacal laughter, she heard a frantic banging at the throne room door, and a girl's voice erupted in a prayer. "Lord, send someone! I can't get inside!"

Griselda's voice, Hannah thought wildly.

A thunderous flapping of wings was heard. A blood-curdling scream was followed by a popping sound.

"Queen Salak! My leg! My leg!" Aufeld bellowed.

Salak was ranting in an incoherent babble. Hannah felt someone grab hold of her arm and drag her away from the room.

"Come. This way!" The voice was deep and resonant. Hannah's head was spinning. "I'll take you with me."

"W-Who are you?" she squeaked.

"Brimral. No talking now. Here. This will help you rest." A fragrant cup was placed to Hannah's lips. A gentle hand held the back of her neck as a warm, creamy liquid was poured down her throat.

Gradually, Hannah's jumbled brain relaxed. "I'll have to carry you. Can you trust me?" Hannah managed to nod. As she was lifted by strong arms, she sank into a heavy sleep.

In the throne room, Salak's mind whirled with anger. She sat quivering. Aufeld lay limp and lifeless at her feet.

When the Eaglia had appeared out of nowhere, Salak had had the presence of mind to change into her serpent form. Of course, she'd bitten Aufeld, sending her lethal poison through his body. It served him right for failing her. Now he'd make a perfect meal!

She raised her hand, pointing it at the corpse. A black crow fluttered from the lifeless body. Flapping its wings, it peered around confusedly with soot-black eyes.

Like lightning, Salak transformed into a serpent. Fixing her bulbous eyes upon the crow, she watched as it stopped trying to fly, its heart beginning to pound in terror. The snake's body whipped forward as if propelled by metal springs, ensnaring the crow with alarming swiftness. The serpent slowly prepared to devour its prize.

When her appetite was sated, the queen returned to her throne. All of her servants came to this same end, and she allowed herself a few moments to gloat over her newest victim.

Now back to business! she thought darkly

Peering in her mirror, she saw the Eaglia carrying the sleeping Hannah through Crimilia to Marigold's hut. Seething, Salak sent her left hand through the glass of the mirror, causing a shower of sparks to fill the room. The glass, instead of falling to the floor in shards, disintegrated into a black powder that hovered in the air.

Salak smiled in glee. "Go," she intoned. "Fill all of Crimilia! Infect the Imperialites. Reek havoc as in the days of old!"

She waved her hand, and the powder glittered as it flowed from the room.

From the palace hallway, Salak heard a shriek, a gurgling cry, and a thud.

She rose and stepped onto the threshold of the room. Griselda lay at an odd angle, her eyes glazed. She writhed in pain. On her forehead, the imprint of the Imperial Lord's Mark shone.

"Traitor!" Salak fumed. Holding out her hand, she pointed an accusing finger at the writhing girl. Instantly, a starling fluttered into the air. Salak grabbed the struggling bird and clawed a crimson-colored nail through its eyes. The bird cheeped in pain. Salak flung the helpless creature to the ground.

"One can never have enough trophies," she gloated. Griselda no longer belonged to her, so she couldn't kill her. However, she could inflict as much pain as possible.

Griselda would be the first in a long line of new trophies to add to her collection. Salak had infected Crimilia with the Senual Plague when Jamal was a little boy of five. Numerous people had died including Marigold's husband, Joakim. Of course, Jamal hadn't been infected! Curse him! Many Imperialites had come to the palace, pleading for mercy. She'd been more than reasonable, offering them freedom, even offering to lift the plague if they'd only serve her. Some had agreed, but the stubborn ones filled the cages in the palace hallways. Now, even more people would pay for their defiance!

Snapping her fingers, she watched a metal cage wrap itself around the newly acquired trophy. Lifting the cage, she placed it in an available aperture.

Smiling in satisfaction, Salak glided back into her throne room. It would soon be time for her to locate Jamal and see what he was up to.

She approached her throne. Her shattered mirror had healed itself. Clear, translucent glass shone brightly, reflecting its creator's distorted face. The mirror waited, ready to show its mistress whatever she wished.

Peering fixedly into the glass, she intoned some words. Soon, Madeleine entered the throne room. "Yes, Your Majesty?" she asked.

"Hannah has been taken. You are a loyal servant, and I need your help," she smiled. "I'll make it worth your while."

deliverance and desolation

"Brandon, please bring me some cloths." Marigold's voice was thin with fatigue.

Brandon hurried to obey. His head was pounding, and he felt weak.

Marigold's hut was jammed with people. Most of them lay, some unconscious, others writhing in pain. The smell of sickness was thick upon the air.

Brandon handed Marigold the cloths. She began swabbing burning foreheads.

Brandon and a few other people, Jamal included, brought bowls of broth and slices of bread to those who were awake.

Since the Senual Plague had begun a month ago, people were coming to Marigold's hut in droves. The hut was now a quarantine establishment. Brandon was surprised that he hadn't been sick.

"Lad?" The familiar voice of Mendel, now weakened, called from a cot in the corner. He and Ursula had arrived only that morning. Usually one who was infected had little hope of survival, but with Jamal staying at the hut, many people had found strength to come to him. Jamal circulated around the room, touching each person and speaking healing to all who asked for it.

"Yes, Mendel?" Brandon asked.

"The young lass is in the bakery kneading the dough. Do you think she would like some soup?"

Brandon smiled to himself. It was so like Mendel to think of others before himself.

"I'll go and see, Mendel."

Brandon thought back to a month previously. He had gone outside for some water and discovered Hannah lying asleep by Jamal's bakery. Relief had flooded through him at the sight of her.

After Hannah had awakened, Jamal had gone to her. Brandon wasn't sure what had happened, but he knew Hannah had tasted Jamal's bread. The change in her was unbelievable! Since she'd arrived, Hannah had worked tirelessly. It was almost as if she feared to stop performing tasks. She'd asked Jamal if she could help with the bread preparation. Of course, he'd given his consent.

Now, Brandon hurried to the back of the hut. He carried a cup of broth. "Hannah? Are you all right?"

Hannah stood at Jamal's workbench. She busily rotated her hands in the dough, massaging it repeatedly. A look of wonder filled her face.

"I'm fine, Brandon," she said. "Have more people come?"

"Yes. The people I told you about who rescued me from Salak's attackers—Samenal, Lydia, and Barson. They came an hour ago. Look, I brought you some soup."

"Thanks." Gratefully, Hannah sank down onto a stool. She guzzled the soup greedily. "I wanna go home, Brandon," she suddenly blurted.

Brandon didn't answer. Instead, he touched Hannah's shoulder. He knew she didn't want him to say anything. She just wanted to talk.

"Feel this dough, Brandon," she said.

Bewildered, Brandon ran his fingers along the mass of bread dough. The dough was smooth and translucent. Golden light seemed to flow from it.

"Pick it up." Hannah instructed.

Brandon lifted the dough. It was light as a feather. He set it back down on the bench. "What did you want me to do that for?" he asked.

Hannah gasped as if she were trying not to cry. "When I worked in the scullery, the bread dough was heavy. It hurt my arms to lift it. This dough is easy to shape. It's light. I don't feel like I'm working at all."

"But you are," Brandon pointed out. "We need your help. The bread gives people strength."

"I don't belong here," Hannah stated simply. "Sometimes, I seem to hear the queen's voice calling to me. Then, I remember what Jamal gave me. Brandon, I feel like I'm suffocating. How can we get home?"

Brandon shook his head. "I don't know," he admitted. "I think we were sent here for some reason."

Hannah nodded. "Me too. I just wish I knew what it was." She thought about the longolia that Jamal had given her. She missed playing it, but she couldn't understand why it bothered her so much.

"I don't care what you say, Jamal!" a harsh voice outside the bakery snapped. Both teenagers recognized the voice of Marshall. "You're going to get us into trouble! I heard Parker in the marketplace yesterday. He claims you are impure because you touch those who are infected with the plague."

"I'm going to the banquet at Annis' tonight," Jamal said calmly. "I'm sure they'll ask me about it there."

"Please, Jamal! Think of us! You're giving our family a bad name!"

"My mission is more important than my name. I must go check on the bread."

"You're impossible!" Marshall stamped away angrily.

Jamal entered the bakery. His face wore a crestfallen expression. "Excellent work," Jamal said.

"Is everyone all right?" Hannah asked.

"Oh, yes. Most of them are asleep. I just came to check on you. I'm off to the house of Annis."

Brandon remembered the conversation between Parker and Annis the night of Patricia's wedding. "Why are you going there?" he asked.

"Because I've been invited for dinner. I'll be back before nightfall. If anyone comes seeking me, please tell them where I am."

Both Brandon and Hannah nodded. Then Jamal left the bakery.

"Something strange is going on," Brandon said. "Annis doesn't like Jamal. Why would he invite him for dinner?"

Hannah shrugged. "I better get back to work," she said.

"We've worked all day," Brandon said. "I don't like the sound of this dinner invitation." He knitted his brow in deep thought.

"Well, then, let's follow him," Hannah said.

"What?" Brandon asked.

"Let's go with him. We'll be there if anything happens."

Brandon thought for a moment; then he nodded.

The streets of Crimilia thronged with people. Brandon and Hannah found it easy to blend into the crowds. They followed Jamal as he strolled along. Often, he waved and shouted a cheerful greeting to a passerby.

Many people flocked to him. Some of them were pale from the sickness of the Senual Plague. Others had skin diseases and any other number of illnesses.

Brandon watched in fascination as the people pled for healing. Jamal honored all of the requests. Brandon described these wondrous signs to Hannah.

Hannah reached down and touched Brandon's bad leg. "Have you thought of asking him for help?" she asked.

"Yes," Brandon admitted. "I just haven't had the nerve."

Hannah nodded in understanding. "He asked me once if I believed he could heal me. I said no. Now, I'm not sure."

"I know he could, and I'd give anything to be able to walk right again," Brandon said. "I just don't know what people would say when we got back home!"

For the first time in weeks, Hannah laughed aloud. Then, her face fell. "Brandon, how come you weren't angry about the accident?" The question burst forth like fizz erupting from a shaken Coke bottle.

Brandon stared at Hannah. "Angry? Of course I was angry. I just—" His voice trailed away. Then, he squeezed Hannah's hand. "I admire you, you know that? You never hide your feelings. When I was little, Dad told me to be strong before he left. I've always tried to do what he said."

"Your dad left, too?"

"Yes. He died from pneumonia."

After a long silence, Hannah squeezed Brandon's hand. They continued to follow Jamal. There seemed no more need to talk for a while.

Suddenly, Jamal stopped walking. A young woman had rushed up to him. She wore a lavish robe. Her face was flushed, and her eyes were red. "Baker!" she cried, "My little girl! She's been struck with the Sensual Plague! I've heard of the wonders that you can do! Please come and help her!"

"You, Jumria?" a scathing female voice called from the crowd. "You're not one of us. You rob us all! Leave us in peace!"

Jamal ignored the outburst. "I was sent only to the Imperialites," he said simply.

Jumria nodded. "But she is only five. She doesn't deserve to die."

"It is not right to take the cakes from the King's children and give them to the peasant's dogs," Jamal said.

Hannah gasped. "What's he doing?" she asked.

Brandon too was thunderstruck. Many of the people in the crowd were nodding in agreement with Jamal's words.

Jumria flinched, but she stared determinedly into his eyes. "What you say is true," she said, "but even the peasant's dogs are given tidbits from a kind King's table."

Jamal beamed. He patted the woman's shoulder. "You have great faith. Go on your way. Your daughter is now well." He looked at the people around him with a mild reproach. Some of them lowered their heads in shame.

The woman's face shone with relief and thanksgiving. "You are the Deliverer!" she cried in ecstasy. "The one the prophecies tell about! I have been in Salak's service for years, but now I know what a fool I was!"

"Hold your tongue, woman!" a familiar voice cried. "You dare to utter blasphemous words? Our Deliverer will be a conquering king! He's only a baker!"

Brandon recognized the deep voice of Parker. In spite of himself, he shuddered.

Jumria did not respond to the outburst. She simply walked away.

Jamal continued walking with Brandon and Hannah following close behind.

"What did that woman mean when she said that Jumria robbed us all?" Brandon wondered aloud.

"She's a tax collector," Hannah explained. "She had dinner at the palace lots of times. I remember her because she always requested goats' milk cheese with her bread."

"Look. I think we're here," Brandon said.

Jamal stopped before an impressive-looking dwelling. Marble pillars supported a lavish home made of brick. Brandon noticed that Parker had also stopped before the mansion.

"Well, baker. I see we're both invited," he said haughtily. Pushing past Jamal, he knocked loudly on the door. Quickly, Brandon and Hannah ducked behind one of the pillars.

A slim young maid opened the door.

"Take me in to Annis!" Parker said grandly.

"Of course. This way, sir," the maid said.

"How are you today?" Jamal asked the maid politely as he began to follow them inside. The maid held up her hand. "I'm sorry, sir. Were you invited to the meal? I'm not authorized—"

"Thank you, Amy," a jovial voice called. "He was invited, as a matter of fact." Brandon recognized the voice of Annis. Now it had a slightly condescending note as it addressed Jamal. "Come in, baker!"

The door closed behind the group.

"What do we do now?" Hannah asked.

"One of us should probably go inside," Brandon said.

"I can't," Hannah said. "My cane'll make too much noise."

Brandon nodded. "Stay down here," he said. "I'll go inside just to check. Then I'll come back out."

Brandon tiptoed up to the immense doors. He tried the knob. To his surprise, the door opened.

Brandon crept down a large, marble-floored hallway. His brace clanked on the floor, and he tried to walk softly.

The murmur of voices led him to a lavish banquet hall. Richly dressed men sat around a large table. Jamal looked plain and unimpressive among the richly appareled men. The smells of roasted chicken, mashed potatoes and gravy, and wine filled the air. Brandon's mouth began to water.

"So, baker," Annis was asking, "you maintain that it's lawful to associate with those contaminated with the Senual Plague? Doesn't that view go against our laws? I understand your mother has opened a quarantine hut. Have you both gone through the required Purification Rites?"

"My mother opens her home to anyone who is in need," Jamal said. "The chicken is delicious!"

"And I understand you have both a blind girl and a crippled boy staying with you who are not of our race? Don't our laws forbid this?"

"The law says nothing of the kind!" Jamal said sharply. "Open your homes to your neighbors who require help," he quoted.

"Exactly," Parker said. "Our neighbors. Clearly, the boy and girl are not Imperialites. They're foreigners."

Jamal did not answer. Brandon's face was flushed with anger.

Suddenly, a familiar figure rushed past him. Brandon had only a moment to register a revealing gown and billowing blonde hair. Angela!

The woman hurried into the banquet hall. Brandon heard Annis issue a muffled curse. The guests gasped in shock when they saw the woman.

"Amy!" he bellowed. "Who's responsible for letting this baggage in?"

Amy, who was passing a platter of smoked fish and a bowl of horseradish sauce around the table, said, "No one knocked, sir. I swear they didn't."

Brandon crept closer to the banquet hall. He peered around the door. Angela knelt at Jamal's feet. In her hand, she clutched a small bottle. Her blonde hair touched the floor, and tears flowed from her eyes.

They fell in cascades onto the dusty, callused feet of the baker. Her body shook with uncontrollable sobs.

Slowly, she unscrewed the cap from her bottle. She gently poured something onto Jamal's feet. A sweet, overpowering fragrance filled the house.

Angela's tears were still flowing unchecked onto Jamal's feet. She hurriedly began to wipe them away with her hair.

Finally, the sobbing ceased, and silence filled the hall. Brandon saw Annis rise angrily.

"Well, intruder, since you've made a complete fool of yourself," he snarled, "you can leave now."

Then Annis turned to Parker and whispered in his ear. Straining to hear, Brandon caught the words: "If this man is who he claims, he'd know very well what trash this woman is! A sinner of the vilest kind!"

"Annis, I have something to tell you," Jamal said.

Annis turned. His face wore a fake smile. "Yes? Tell me," he said.

"There were two men who owed money to a king. One owed fifty shekels of silver and the other owed five hundred. Neither of the men could pay, and the king had compassion on them. The debts were canceled. Tell me, which person will love the king more?"

Annis cleared his throat. Both he and Parker fidgeted nervously.

"Um, I—I suppose the man who owed the most," Annis finally admitted.

Jamal nodded. "You have answered correctly," he said.

Then he turned to Angela, who still huddled on the floor. Her eyes stared defiantly at the richly dressed men; then she gazed fixedly at Jamal. She seemed to be steeling herself for the embarrassment to come. "Do you see this woman? I came to your house for a meal. You talk constantly about the law, but you did not observe it yourself. You gave me no water to wash the dust of the road from my feet, but this woman washed my feet with her own tears. You did nothing, but this woman gave her most valuable possession to express her love for me."

Annis glared. "Be that as it may, baker, this is a private banquet. She was not invited."

Ignoring Annis's words, Jamal smiled at Angela. "Daughter, your sins are forgiven you. Go in peace."

"What?" Parker roared. "You dare presume that you can forgive sins?"

Jamal continued to observe Angela. "You are forgiven," he repeated. "Go and leave Salak's service."

"Blasphemer!" Annis raged. He brought his fist down on the table and upset the bowl of horseradish.

Amy quickly entered to clean up, but Jamal shook his head. Calmly, he used his own napkin to mop up the spill. "If any of you men have no sin on your conscience, throw her out and perform the usual penalty of stoning," he said.

The guests sat absolutely still. Their eyes strayed to Angela, then to each other. Brandon suddenly realized with a jolt of shock that all the men knew Angela very well.

Rising to their feet, they shot looks of pure venom at Jamal and swept from the room.

"Thank you," Angela whispered. Her voice was choked.

"I do not condemn you, Angela," Jamal said. "Go and sin no more."

Slowly, Angela rose and left the room. Jamal finished cleaning up the spilled horseradish. Then he walked out into the hall.

"Brandon?" he called. "You can come out now." His eyes twinkled.

Startled, Brandon stood. Jamal grinned at him. "You took a risk, Brandon," he said. "I'm glad you're here, even if you'd been safer staying at the hut. I have something to give you."

So saying, Jamal withdrew a plain wooden paintbrush and a small roll of parchment from the folds of his robe. "This is a Trinimal Brush. All the colors of creation are contained within it."

Brandon blinked in surprise. "How did you know?" he whispered.

"That you were interested in painting? I have seen how you observe landscapes and people. You have the artist's ability to find truth and present it to the world. Just as Hannah neglected her talent because of bitterness, you have buried yours because of the fear of rejection."

"Do you know what kids at school will say to me?"

Jamal smiled at him. "You don't have to use the supplies. Just keep them as souvenirs of your time here.

I just want you to acknowledge that you have talent. That is all. Come on. Let's get back to Mother's hut! I'm still hungry, aren't you?"

Brandon tentatively took the Trinimal Brush and parchment from the baker's hands and placed them in his pants' pocket. He smiled sheepishly and changed the subject. "It wasn't much of a meal for you, was it?" he asked.

Jamal laughed. "Those meals never are. The leaders of the Imperialites have become poisoned with their own pride. They've contracted a worser illness than Senual Plague. They have Salak's disease. I've dealt with their contempt since I was old enough to talk."

Brandon followed Jamal outside. "Hannah's waiting for us," he said.

The moon was shining brightly, and the air was fragrant and slightly cool. "We're ready to go, Hannah," Brandon called.

There was no answer except the singing of crickets.

Dread suddenly slammed into Brandon's stomach. "Hannah?" he called. "Where are you?"

Jamal began to search along the ground. He looked behind the pillars of Annis' dwelling. His face became stony.

"Come, Brandon," he said softly. "We must go."

"What? What is it?" Brandon cried.

"She's been taken to Plenty Palace once again. The time has come."

"Come? Come for what?"

Jamal did not answer. Instead, he gestured to the ground behind the pillars. A scarlet snake skin, grotesque and empty, lay shining in the moonlight.

Surprisingly, it was not this grisly sight that struck terror into Brandon's heart. It was the object that lay beside it. Hannah's cane, abandoned and bent, lay in the dewy grass.

Squaring his shoulders, Brandon faced Jamal. "What do we do?" he asked.

"We go to get her," Jamal said simply.

drudgery once again

"I want her to hurt!" Salak's voice rumbled. She sat on her throne and glared at Madeleine. "Do you understand me? Inflict severe pain on her! No leniency will be tolerated!"

Madeleine nodded. Her face was expressionless. She looked weary of the whole world. "Your Majesty? What should I do to her?"

"Force her to prepare the Special Bread." Salak grinned savagely. Her voice was no longer loud, but it was icy. "Stand over her the whole time. Beat her if necessary. Fifty loaves must be made. When she is finished, take her back to the dungeon. She is forbidden to eat."

Madeleine nodded. "Your Majesty? I haven't been paid yet for telling you about the baker's dinner invitation with the Imperialite official. I thought our agreement was—"

Salak glared. "You'll receive your reward when I say you will! Now get out!"

Trembling, Madeleine scurried from the throne room.

On the threshold, she saw two distinguished-looking men. Of course, they didn't acknowledge her.

Annis and Parker stormed into the room. "That insufferable lout, Jamal!" Parker raged. "He must die! You promised us—"

Salak rose. She fixed a steely gaze on both men. "Have you forgotten who you're addressing?" she hissed. "I'm ruler of Crimilia! You answer to me!"

Parker stepped back, and Annis hastened to explain. "Forgive our ill conduct, Your Majesty. It's just that this uppity baker is causing trouble for our people. He stirs up the crowds. They no longer listen to us."

"Well, of course he does," Salak said reasonably. "He's a troublemaker, after all. What do you want me to do?"

"Help us make an example of him," Annis said. "Like you promised when we entered your service. You promised us prestige and wealth. Well, you've provided that, of course. Now, we—"

"You want the baker to die. Is that it?" Salak asked calmly.

Parker shifted his weight from one foot to the other. "Um, well, you see, for the good of the people—"

Salak laughed. "Don't be coy, Parker. I know you too well." She lightly caressed his hand. "The desire for power is nothing to be ashamed of. Only those who do not desire it are fools. I have not forgotten my promise. You will continue to be the rulers of the Imperialite nation. The baker will be taken care of."

Annis and Parker smiled with relief. "Thank you, my queen. Forgive our intrusion," Annis said. "Come, Parker."

The two men strolled toward the door.

"Oh, you two?" Salak called playfully.

The men turned around.

"The baker will be taken care of tomorrow at noon. Come and bring the other rulers of the law. You wouldn't want to miss the show, would you? You have a vital part to play."

"Of course, Your Majesty. Thank you."

When the men had gone, Salak smiled in euphoric rapture. Fools! All of them were gullible fools from the most insignificant scullery maid to the highest-ranking Imperialite official. They all were her tools to manipulate and use. She especially loved using the Imperialite rulers. They were her best weapons.

Once again, she congratulated herself on taking Hannah captive. The girl would never escape, and soon Jamal would be at her mercy.

"Get moving you oaf!" Madeleine screeched.

Feeling dazed and dizzy, Hannah staggered into the scullery. Without her cane, she was totally lost. She groped along the right-hand wall as Madeleine pushed her from behind.

"Don't push so hard!" Hannah cried. "I can't walk very fast. I feel sick."

"I don't care how you feel!" Madeleine screeched. "You have a job to do."

Madeleine positioned Hannah in front of the kneading trough. Hannah gasped. A putrid smell attacked her nostrils. "What is that?" she sputtered.

"It's bread dough. You must knead it for an hour."

"A whole hour?"

Madeleine slapped her face with such suddenness that Hannah didn't even cry out. "Yes, an hour! Now get going!"

Sighing, Hannah placed her hands into the trough. As she remembered from her month in the scullery, the bread dough was extremely heavy. For a moment, she thought about the dough in Jamal's bakery—its lightness, the ease of kneading.

The dough in the trough clung to her hands in sticky clumps. It contained sharp shards of some strange substance that gouged her knuckles.

As Hannah worked, she became aware of a burning sensation in her hands. She'd never experienced anything like it.

After a few moments, she stopped kneading. She was about to take her hands from the trough, when Madeleine slapped her once again. "Keep working," she snarled.

"What's with you?" Hannah asked.

"I'll slap you again!"

Hannah hurriedly began her never-ending task. Her hands felt raw and weak. The smell from the trough made her even queasier than she already was. She didn't know what on earth was happening, but she knew she'd never taste this bread. She couldn't imagine what kind it was.

At long last, she finished kneading and was instructed to shape the bread into loaves. Usually, this task was very easy, but this dough wouldn't cooperate. It kept breaking apart every time she tried to shape it.

"Problem?" Madeleine mocked.

"My only problem is you!" Hannah snapped.

Madeleine seized Hannah's hair so ferociously that the girl couldn't contain a scream of pain. She jerked the hair savagely and lowered Hannah's head toward the trough. The smell became overpowering.

"Please, I'm sorry. I didn't mean—" Hannah gasped.

"Shut up!" Hannah could feel the hands gripping her hair begin to tremble. "You think you're so high and mighty just because you went to see *him?* Griselda thought so, too. She changed the first day he arrived. Her Majesty sent her down to the dungeon with some cakes for him."

Hannah didn't say anything. She was afraid Madeleine would push her face into the disgusting dough. The grip on her hair had loosened slightly, and she wanted to keep it that way.

"She sent me to that troublemaker to collect his trays. He never ate anything. My family goes hungry everyday. He just sat there looking superior. He told me that he could give me something more substantial than what Her Majesty offers."

Madeleine snorted with contempt. "What does *he* know about it? Griselda might have been taken in but not me! Work for whatever you can get. It's how you survive!"

"Is that what your family told you before they sent you away?" The words were out before Hannah could stop herself.

There was a long pause. Madeleine released Hannah's hair. "They said what was true. How *else* can you live in this place? Griselda didn't play by the rules, and now she's gone." The voice trembled, and Madeleine roughly thrust Hannah against the trough. "Now, get back to work!"

At last, fifty loaves were placed on the scullery table. Hannah was so exhausted, she didn't even protest when she was led to the dungeon. She would gladly eat a slice of that bread so that she could have some energy.

"You'll stay in here until tomorrow," Madeleine said.

Hannah was shoved into the same cell Jamal had occupied. She crumpled to the ground and immediately fell into a deep sleep.

the capture

At Marigold's hut, Brandon stood beside Mendel's cot. "How are you and Ursula?" he asked.

"Much better, lad," Mendel reassured him.

"Look, Hannah has been taken. Jamal and I are going to try and get her. I just wanted to—"

Mendel rose shakily to his feet. "Say no more, Brandon. I'm coming too."

"And I," Ursula said.

"No," Brandon said. "You're needed here."

"No arguments," Ursula said. "Where Jamal goes, we go."

"Us too," Barson said. He, Lydia, and Samenal had also risen from their cots.

Brandon nodded to them all. "I'll go tell Jamal. We'll be heading out in a few minutes."

In the bakery, Jamal and Marigold clung together in a fierce embrace. "My son, not yet. Please." Her voice was choked with sobs. "I can't lose you."

Jamal did not answer. Tears flowed from his eyes.

"I remember when you were four years old. You were playing beside this very shop when a snake bit you on the hand. How you cried! But I held you and said I would always be there to protect you." Her face crumpled.

"But everything was all right, wasn't it?" Jamal sought to bring comfort to the woman who had given him so much.

Marigold smiled. "Salak had no effect on you. Even as a serpent, her venom did not work."

"Her time has come, Mother. I must go." He broke down suddenly, and she cradled the tall man in her arms.

Movement at the bakery entrance alerted them both. Marshall stood awkwardly, his face red. He held out a tentative hand toward his half-brother. "I don't approve of what you're doing," he said simply. "If you'd stayed at home and earned a living, we'd all be safe. I know I'm always complaining, but you're my brother. I love you even if you are exasperating. The Imperial Lord go with you."

Jamal smiled through his tears. "I've left some honey cakes for you. You always did eat them all before I even got one!" he laughed. The familiar twinkle shone briefly in his eyes. "Please look after Mother," he said.

Outside, a small group gathered. Brandon stood in front; Mendel and Ursula were next, and Barson, Samenal, and Lydia were last.

"They all wanted to come," Brandon explained.

Jamal nodded. "Thank you," he said.

Samenal looked at Jamal's face. "For years, I was bitter because Lydia and I lost our three children to the Senual Plague. When you started performing miracles of healing as a young man, I was resentful. I thought you should have saved my children. Now I've seen you heal so many with the plague. No one can do all that you do except he come from the Imperial Lord. You are the true Deliverer."

Jamal beamed.

Brandon squared his shoulders. Fear gripped his stomach, but he began walking toward the perilous journey ahead. The others followed close behind.

The stars shone brightly in the clear sky. Brandon and the others walked doggedly along, their feet rustling in the grass.

"We'll stop here for the night," Jamal said.

Everyone nodded gratefully. They were in a wooded area with many trees and plants.

Jamal opened a paper-wrapped bundle and began passing out bread and apples. He did not take a seat until everyone was served.

"I would have been glad to serve the meal," Ursula pointed out.

Jamal smiled at her. "No. I came to be a servant. Now let's eat. I'm hungry."

After the meal, Jamal reached into the pocket of his robe. He withdrew a small cloth package. "Watch carefully," he instructed.

Brandon leaned forward and saw Jamal unwrap the bundle. Seven red seeds nestled in the cloth.

Jamal gently shook the seeds out onto the ground. Immediately, they sank into the rich soil.

Brandon watched, fascinated, as the ground where the seeds had fallen began to pulsate with dazzling light. He noticed that the others were slack-jawed with surprise.

A large tree broke through the rich soil. Multiple branches groaned under the weight of white blossoms. "The Tree of Memorium," Jamal explained. "Watch."

With a resounding pop, the blossoms broke open. Large, crimson fruits burst onto the branches. The fruits were so ripe that rich juice could be seen hovering in the round globes, and a citrusy fragrance filled the air. The branches quivered as if their occupants wanted to jump from the tree into waiting hands. "What are they?" Brandon gasped.

"Memorium Fruits," Jamal said. "The tree and its fruit will remain here forever. It is a symbol of my life which I give that you may live. When you partake of the juice from the Memorium, remember what I have done for you."

Jamal plucked one of the vibrant fruits and squeezed its crimson juice into a cup. Slowly, he passed the cup to each person. Bewildered, they partook of the offering. Brandon took a tentative sip and grimaced. The juice was very bitter when it first entered his mouth. He wanted to spit it out. Then, the bitter taste was replaced by an extraordinary sweetness.

Jamal was the last person to drink.

Brandon noticed that Jamal's face was haggard and strained. As Jamal raised the cup to his lips, his hands shook.

"Shouldn't we all get some rest?" Lydia asked.

Jamal rose shakily to his feet. "Yes," he said. "Of course."

Then, nodding to Mendel, Barson, and Samenal, he gestured to a grove of cherry trees several yards away. "Will you three come with me, please?" he requested.

The men stood up and followed Jamal into the grove. Brandon heard Jamal instructing them: "Stay here and keep watch. Pray. I am going to do the same."

Brandon began helping Ursula and Lydia to clear away the meal wrappings. "I don't know what the matter is with him tonight," Ursula said.

"Yes," Lydia pointed out. "He's looking quite pale. I hope he's not becoming infected with the plague."

Brandon shuddered. A desire to check on Jamal surged through him.

Quickly, he darted into the grove of cherry trees. He found Samenal, Mendel, and Barson huddled on the ground. They were fast asleep. Of course, Brandon wasn't surprised. All of them had walked a long way.

Where was Jamal? Brandon tiptoed farther into the trees. Suddenly, he heard guttural sobbing.

"Papa, if there's any other way, please take this burden from me! Please don't make me eat Salak's bread! Yet, not what I will, but what you will I'll do."

Brandon's heart began to pound. That was Jamal's voice! What on earth was he talking about?

Jamal began stumbling toward the three men who were asleep. Brandon saw him gaze at them with compassion and sadness. "Couldn't you have watched for a little while?" he asked them. "Wake up! Pray that you'll be safe."

Jamal walked back into the grove. Brandon heard his sobs grow even more uncontrolled.

Without stopping to think, he burst into the grove and stared in shock. His stomach convulsed.

Jamal sprawled on the ground, his eyes bloodshot and his body shaking. His skin was white, and blood-red sweat droplets coursed down his forehead.

"Jamal!" Brandon cried.

Jamal raised his head. "Thank you for your concern, Brandon, but you must leave this clearing. It's not safe."

"Why? What's the mat—"

Out of the darkness, a crimson shape materialized. Brandon just had a second to realize that the shape was a snake when a piercing pain shot through his left hand. The serpent's fangs had pierced his skin!

Brandon screamed. His vision became foggy.

"Salak!" a voice roared. "Leave him be! I'm coming willingly."

The serpent had vanished. The queen, dressed in the same apricot-colored, jewel-encrusted gown she'd worn on the day she'd seduced Evelina, stood before Jamal. "You're such a fool," she whispered. "It's my day now. I'll do what I please and hurt whomever I please."

She grabbed Jamal's arm and propelled him forward. Her eyes glowed crimson with triumph.

As Jamal was led from the grove, he bestowed a piercing look upon Brandon's face. Brandon blinked. His vision was slowly returning! What was going on?

Before his eyes, the fang marks were disappearing! Strength was seeping back into his limbs!

Tears filled Brandon's eyes. Even while Jamal was being led away, he'd healed him.

Struggling to his feet, Brandon hobbled toward the sleeping men. "Come on!" he cried, "It's an emergency!"

the bread of scorn

"All right! Wake up!" Madeleine's voice echoed in the damp, cold dungeon. "We'll have lots of guests today. Get moving!"

Quivering with weakness, Hannah struggled to sit up. "Please," she croaked, "could I have some—"

"Shut up! We've got things to make!"

Stumbling, Hannah allowed herself to be pushed up the dungeon stairs. The thought of making even more bread filled her with revulsion.

In the scullery, the other girls were busy. Hannah could smell pies and cakes baking. Her stomach growled.

Madeleine shoved her against the butter churn. "There'll be a feast today," she said. "You'll churn five different batches of cream."

Hannah cringed. Her arms were too heavy to lift. She knew that Madeleine was standing over her.

"Get moving," Madeleine snarled.

The morning dragged by at a snail's pace. The cream took forever to thicken, and Hannah was starving!

After what seemed like an eternity, Madeleine wrenched the churn handle from her grasp. "That's all for today," she snapped. "Come on. The show's about to start."

"Show? What—"

"An execution of a troublemaker. Her Majesty wanted all of us to be there."

Hannah would have gladly chosen to stay in the dungeon. At least there she could have gotten some sleep! But now she was pushed outside into overpowering sunlight. Hannah stumbled backward. Her head began to ache.

"Come on, Ox," Madeleine grouched.

Hannah stumbled along until they reached the front of the palace. Deafening chatter filled the air. Hannah could smell the pies and cakes that were baked earlier in the day. She also smelled roasted meats and wines. People rushed by her, jostling her as they passed. The mood was a festive one.

"Her Majesty always provides the best feasts on execution days!" Hannah heard a woman tell someone. "I wonder how long the criminal will last."

As the people surged around her, Hannah became aware that Madeleine was no longer holding her shoulders. Had she left her alone? Panic surged through her. She hated being with Madeleine, but she didn't have her cane. She was totally alone.

A hand grabbed Hannah's arm, and she screamed.

"Shhh!" a familiar voice hissed. "You wanna get us killed?"

"Brandon!" Hannah cried. "What—"

"Never mind how I got here! We hafta stop this! Mendel, Barson, and Samenal saw the crowd and ran away! Samenal said something about gathering re-enforcements, but I don't believe him. I don't know where Ursula and—"

Suddenly, silence fell on the crowd.

"All kneel before Her Royal Majesty, Queen Lucinda!" a reverberating voice thundered.

Hannah could hear people shuffling and falling to their knees. Biting her lip, she stood straight and tall. She felt Brandon's hand grasp hers.

"You five!" the echoing voice screamed. "Show some respect for your queen!"

Five? Hannah wondered. Feeling suddenly braver, she shouted defiantly, "She's not our queen!"

Gasps echoed around the courtyard. Brandon saw the soldier who had given the order fidget nervously. He looked to where Queen Salak lay on a jeweled litter carried by five men. She was breathtakingly beautiful, but Brandon felt only sickness as he stared at her stony face.

The soldier leaned forward and whispered to the queen. She looked at Brandon with shock and hatred; then her eyes turned to Hannah. Contempt shone from them.

"Never mind, Bovril," she said. "There are more important things to tend to."

"Yes, my queen," Bovril said.

"My loyal subjects!" Salak called. "Today you will witness the downfall of one of the worst evildoers in our land. He spreads lies and contaminates what we hold dear. A sniveling baker who has little regard for our society."

"That's a lie!" Hannah blurted. Shocked at her daring, she continued, "He's healed people of their injuries and provided food to those who could not afford it."

"Silence!" Salak bellowed. "He claims that seeking pleasure is evil! I have built a society upon freedom and liberty! Everyone can fulfill any appetites they may have. There is no shame in that. He refuses to conform to the rules of our society."

Murmurs of consternation filled the courtyard. A familiar voice spoke up from the crowd. "He talks of uprising!" Parker called. "He claims to be a Deliverer."

"He claims to be the only person who provides true freedom," Annis' voice rang out. "I ask all of you, what do we lack? Are we not all well provided for? Those of us who keep the law and obey authority are protected."

"Yeah, and everyone else is killed!" Brandon called. "What kind of ruler is that?"

Salak's face was crimson with rage. "Bring those two infidels to me! And bring the prisoner's mother!"

Two men from the watching crowd grabbed Brandon and Hannah. They pushed them to the litter. Brandon's eyes opened in surprise. Ursula and Lydia were bringing Marigold to the front of the crowd. Lydia and Ursula looked straight into the crazed eyes of the queen. "We'll not leave her," Ursula said.

Salak glared at them all. She leaned forward and whispered gloatingly, "You'll be the first people to witness his downfall. Of course, you'll die afterwards. Marigold! So glad you could come! Were my soldiers kind when they fetched you? Your less-important son left you to their mercy, didn't he? How does it feel to be abandoned?" She bestowed a look of hatred on the stricken mother. "Bring the prisoner out!"

A clanking of chains followed this command. Jamal, his body bent and bloody, was pushed into the center of the crowd. "He's received the required one hundred lashes, Your Majesty," Bovril said.

Salak grinned. "Well, Jamal? You are charged with inciting rebellion and blasphemy. The required punishment is death. Do you have anything to say before your sentence is carried out?" Her voice was filled with mockery.

Jamal's eyes surveyed the large crowd. Many people were eating and chatting. They did not look at him.

"Father, please forgive them." Jamal's voice was soft, but it echoed around the courtyard. "They are all being used."

Salak grinned at him. "Is that all you have to say?"

Jamal nodded.

"Very well, then. Let the execution commence. Bring out the Bread of Scorn!"

Standing beside Brandon, Hannah clutched his hand. "What can we do?" she whispered desperately.

"I don't know," Brandon admitted.

Brandon watched as a teenage girl brought a large platter of bread and placed it into Salak's hands.

"Well done, Madeleine." The queen touched the girl's arm. Beside him, Hannah gasped. "According to law, each person must come forward and feed the prisoner," Salak said. "Form a line and begin."

The people quickly finished their meals. Then, like an assembly line at a factory, they all approached the platter of bread. Each person took a slice and hurried toward Jamal. The people began shoving the slices of bread into his mouth.

Jamal accepted each piece and chewed with determination.

As he chewed, Brandon noticed that his body was starting to convulse. At one point, he swallowed a slice of bread and groaned with pain.

Soon, the scene turned nightmarish. The people came at Jamal from every direction. He would barely have one slice swallowed when another would be shoved into his mouth.

The baker fell to the ground, the chains cutting into his limbs. His face flushed crimson with fever, and his body shook with spasms. Still, the bread kept coming.

"Stop!" Brandon screamed. "Please!"

Salak raised a hand. "The rebellious ones haven't had their turn yet. Move aside so they can reach the platter." Her eyes gleamed maliciously.

"No!" Hannah screamed as she was jerked forward by a soldier.

Salak laughed at her. "What are you complaining about, slave?" she mocked. "You made this bread, after all. Don't you think it tastes good?"

The fist of shock slammed into Hannah's heart. The soldier forced her to grab a slice of bread. As Hannah held the coarse slice, she became aware of the putrid smell that she'd noticed yesterday. Her mother and father's voices filled her mind—their arguments, their bitter words. She heard herself yelling at her mother: "I hate you! You made me this way! You made Daddy leave!"

Shaking with horror, she tried to throw the slice of bread to the ground, but she was pushed forward to the writhing figure.

"Feed him!" Salak raged.

Hannah, her eyes streaming, placed her slice of bread into the open mouth. Her hand brushed against his cheek, and she gasped. His skin was burning hot. Once again, Jamal began to chew.

"I'm sorry. I'm sorry." Hannah choked on her words.

Behind her, Brandon was pushed forward. He placed his slice in Jamal's mouth; then he fell to the ground, covering his face in shame. He saw himself at school, listening to Gordon Hamilton and the other kids tease Hannah.

"She's so fat! She'll never be asked out on a date!"

Brandon said nothing in her defense.

Hannah heard the final group of spectators surge forward and give their grisly offerings. Jamal was screaming. He sounded like a wounded animal. She'd never heard anything so horrible.

From his position on the ground, Brandon watched the helpless victim. Blood and bile were issuing from his mouth. He watched as oozing sores erupted onto the baker's face, arms, and legs. Jamal coughed and gagged.

An eerie silence had come over the courtyard. The people stared down at the suffering baker in wonder. Brandon realized that a thick fog had descended. The sun had completely disappeared, and it was still daytime.

"My Father! My Father!" Jamal wailed. "Why have you left me?"

Brandon saw the queen descend from her litter. Her face was aglow with triumph. She stood before Jamal and stared down at him.

"He's left you because you're weak," she hissed. "I offered you prestige and wealth. You could have had everything! But, no, you fool! Now I'll have my revenge! That bread ate into your very soul! Its acid corrodes your very flesh!" She sent a stream of spittle onto his sore-covered face. Jamal winced with pain, and she laughed. Her laughter was like the howl of a ravenous wolf. "Now who is victorious? I've crushed you, and Crimilia's mine forever!"

Salak threw back her head and shouted defiantly into the air. "What can you do now, my Lord? I've crushed your son! I've made you cry a second time! My joy knows no bounds!"

Once again, she stared in triumph at her weakened enemy. "Good-bye, Jamal!" With that, she shoved the final slice of the Bread of Scorn into the baker's mouth.

Jamal swallowed the final piece of bread. A guttural wail filled the courtyard. Brandon heard several people cry out. He looked and saw Marigold sitting by her son. Lydia and Ursula sat with her.

Suddenly, Jamal raised his head. He appeared to muster some strength as he bestowed upon the queen a piercing stare. Then he surveyed the gathered crowd.

"It is accomplished!" he called.

Then he crumpled to the ground and lay still.

"The upstart is dead!" Salak gloated. Several people cheered.

"Now come into the palace. We will all drink a victory toast to the crushing of rebellion." Then the queen turned to Jamal's corpse. "Throw the body on the garbage heap."

"My queen!" Parker made his way to the front of the crowd. "We must make sure that he is indeed dead."

Salak smiled at him. "You do the honors, Parker."

Parker grinned with relish. He drew a gleaming knife from the belt he wore around his waist. With a vicious thrust, he pierced Jamal's left side. A stream of blood and water gushed forth.

It was at this point that Hannah crumpled to the ground. She knew no more.

From his prostrate position, Brandon saw Salak raise a hand. "Bovril! Take the five troublemakers and place them in the dungeon. They are to be given no food. Their execution will occur tomorrow. Madeleine?"

The girl who'd brought out the bread came to stand before the queen. She was shaking.

Her face wearing a smile of contempt, Salak threw a handful of silver coins at Madeleine's feet. "Your reward, my dear," she mocked. "Now, go make sure there is enough dough to prepare another batch of the Bread of Scorn. It is just what these rebellious people need."

Madeleine looked at the defeated baker. Without warning, she bolted away.

Bovril and some other soldiers surrounded Brandon, Hannah, and the three women.

"One of you, carry the girl," Bovril ordered. He forced Brandon to his feet.

All of them were led into the dank dungeon. After they were shoved into a cell, they crumpled to the ground. Brandon, Marigold, Ursula, and Lydia looked at each other with eyes that were empty—empty of joy and empty of hope. From upstairs, they could hear laughter and the sounds of merry feasting.

Outside, stillness pervaded. Birds did not sing, and the thick fog still enveloped the land. The whole world seemed to be mourning.

From out of a clump of rosebushes that skirted the edge of the courtyard, two women emerged. One was richly dressed, and the other wore plain clothes.

"We can't leave him there," the richly dressed woman made her way to the manacled corpse.

"No," the other woman whispered. "What can we do?"

"I am well off. I have a mausoleum I can place him in on my property. It's the least I can do. He healed my daughter of the plague." The woman broke down as she looked at the fallen Deliverer.

"He healed my soul," the other woman whispered. "I've brought some spices and linens. Help me."

Silently, they began to minister to their savior.

hope returns

By the next morning, the thick fog still had not lifted. In the dungeon, the five prisoners were cramped and weak. Hannah, who had revived soon after being locked up, was the weakest one of all. She hadn't eaten in three days.

"I don't know why I'm complaining," she managed to whisper. "He didn't eat for over a month."

"Was that when he came to the palace the first time?" Brandon asked.

Hannah nodded. "It's my fault he came back." Her face crumpled in sorrow.

Brandon squared his shoulders. "We hafta find a way to get out of here," he said.

"What's the use?" Ursula said bluntly. "We'll be under this harpy queen's rule forever! And my Mendel—" her voice trailed away.

"Marshall didn't abandon me," Marigold suddenly spoke for the first time since their confinement. Her voice was surprisingly strong, even though her face was haggard. "I forced him to stay in the hiding place under the bakery. He might be gathering some helpers."

Out of the darkness, stealthy footsteps were heard. Instantly, the prisoners stiffened.

"Leave us be!" Lydia called. "We've done nothing."

"Shhh," a small, thin voice cautioned. "Be quiet."

"Madeleine?" Hannah blurted in shock. "What're you—"

"Just wait," Madeleine's voice was thin with fatigue and sadness. The prisoners listened in shock as they heard a key being fitted into the cell door. In a moment, the door opened.

"Now get out," Madeleine ordered. "And run."

"Madeleine? You—" Hannah began.

Madeleine began to sob. "I've ruined my life!" she cried. "I'm fifteen, and I still haven't experienced my Moon Phase. Do you have any idea how people treat you if you're different from them? Her Majesty said she'd keep me safe and pay me money if I worked for her as a spy. I was always jealous of the other girls, and I wanted to be noticed. Please, let me do something right for a change! Go!"

The group rushed from the cell. They didn't know where they were going, but they were relieved to be free.

As Hannah walked by their rescuer, she felt something being thrust into her hand—a familiar wooden instrument!

"Take it," Madeleine whispered. "When Griselda disappeared, I went through her things and found this. I'd seen her take it from your room earlier, and I—" she shuddered. "—please take it."

Joy filled Hannah's heart. The longolia! Jamal's gift to her! "Thank you," she whispered. "Come with us. We'll go to Marigold's hut and try to figure something out."

"No," Madeleine spoke flatly. "I don't deserve to come with you."

"I didn't deserve to have a good friend like Jamal," Hannah pointed out. "Please come."

Madeleine shook her head. The group looked at her sadly. Then they left the dungeon.

Flinging the key away, Madeleine entered the prison cell and closed the door behind her.

The morning was damp, and the thick fog still hovered over the land. Angela, clutching a package of myrrh, hurried onto Jumria's property. She approached the mausoleum and stopped dead. The door stood wide open! Swallowing convulsively, she peered into the room. Nothing was there except the chains that had shackled the body. They were broken! The linen cloth that had encased the corpse lay in an odd position, almost like an empty shell. The cloth seemed to hold the imprint of a recent occupant.

A deafening flurry of wings made her gasp. Looking up, Angela saw two strange creatures descending from the sky. They wore snow-white robes. "You seek the Deliverer, the one who was executed," one of the Eaglias called. "He is not here! He is alive! Go, tell Jumria, then both of you find Mendel, Barson, and Samenal. Gather together in the cherry tree grove, and there you will be told what to do."

Her eyes bright with wonder, Angela hurried toward Jumria's house.

In the palace hallway, the blinded birds were continuing their incessant singing. The pitiful music struck sadness into Hannah's heart. She remembered her first day in the palace when she'd attempted to feed the birds and had been caught.

As the group filed past the cages, Hannah suddenly no longer cared what anyone thought of her. She didn't care that the queen would hear the music. She only wanted to bring some light into the tortured and captive birds' lives. She placed the longolia to her lips and began to play with all her might. The music that emanated from the instrument was piercingly sweet.

"Hannah, what're you—" Brandon began.

Hannah didn't stop playing to answer. She played a song she'd learned by listening to Griselda hum—a lilting melody that was joyful and hauntingly sad all at once.

As Hannah played, she became aware that Marigold, Lydia, and Ursula were singing: "Tyranny has chained our land with poison and pain! A Deliverer has come to cleanse every stain! Give the Imperial Lord eternal glory! Blind girl and crippled boy will put an end to Evil's story. Baker will prepare Freedom's Bread in his purifying oven."

Suddenly, Hannah noticed that the birds were silent. She stopped playing and listened closely. It was astonishing how quiet the palace hall had become.

Brandon suddenly gasped. "Ursula! Lydia! Marigold! Look!"

Peering within the cages, the women gasped in wonder.

Before their eyes, the birds' wings were expanding! The clipped feathers that prevented flight were growing back.

"Keep playing, Hannah!" Brandon cried.

Hannah didn't stop to think. She simply obeyed.

Brandon watched in shock as the birds' eyes began to glow. All of the birds began chirping in delight! They frantically flapped their wings!

With a rending crack, all of the cages splintered into fragments. The birds flew in torrents from the wreckage of the cages!

Hannah stopped playing. "What's happening?" she screamed above the cacophony of joyous birdsong.

"You've freed them! Well done!" a reverberating, familiar voice echoed around the palace hallway.

It couldn't be, and yet—

"Jamal!" Hannah cried. She suddenly felt queasy. "I'm hallucinating," she whispered.

But no. Brandon and the women were crying out in joy. Hannah felt a callused hand touch her shoulder. Above her pounding heart, she still heard the joyful music of the birds. "Are you a ghost?" she asked.

Jamal laughed. "Touch my hand," he instructed.

Hannah did so. It was solid. She suddenly was overcome with unsurpassable joy.

Brandon stared in shock at the baker. The man's face, arms, and legs bore scars from the numerous sores that had erupted while he ate the Bread of Scorn. His side still bore the wound inflicted by Parker.

"You're alive!" Brandon stated the obvious in a choked voice.

Jamal threw back his head and laughed a laugh of pure pleasure. "I am indeed! Salak overlooked one essential thing in her plot to conquer Crimilia. When a willing but innocent victim eats the Bread of Scorn, he is poisoned temporarily, but then the bread works against itself. He must die, but the bread provides its own antidote to the poison."

"My son!" Marigold rushed to the baker. For a moment, mother and son clung together in rapture.

Then Jamal looked at the birds. They flocked around him. Some perched on his shoulders and others hovered in the air.

He reached into the folds of his plain white robe, withdrawing a loaf of bread. The loaf shone with a dazzling golden light. Gently, Jamal broke the loaf into pieces. He fed each bird a morsel.

"Hannah?" he said. "Can you begin playing again, please?"

Hannah started playing the same song. An earsplitting crash made her jump.

"Hannah!" Brandon cried. "All the figurines are breaking! The tapestries are crumbling into dust!"

Then, before all of them, the birds began to transform into people. Men, women, and children stood before Jamal. They bowed to him and shouted praises of thanksgiving.

"Hannah! You're all right!" Griselda's voice rang out among the joyous praise.

Hannah was too overcome with happiness to speak.

Jamal withdrew five more loaves from the folds of his robe. He passed them to Brandon, Hannah, Lydia, Ursula, and Marigold.

Hannah explored the loaf with her fingers. It was flat, round, and smooth to the touch. She remembered the bread Jamal had given her before, and anticipation filled her soul. Tentatively, she placed the loaf into her mouth. The bread's taste was similar to a graham cracker, yet it also contained a sharp, slightly bitter tang. Briefly, her mind was wrenched back to the horrifying scene in the courtyard. She heard Jamal's cries and remembered her participation in the execution. Then, just as quickly, the memory faded, and an extraordinary sense of peace filled her.

"Now, come!" Jamal called. "We must all go to the throne room! We have one more thing to tend to."

As the whole company surged down the hallway, Brandon spotted a familiar object lying among the wreckage. The dazzling porcelain bowl! It glimmered with a brilliant light! Brandon reached out and snatched the undamaged object.

"Jamal!" he cried.

Jamal turned and beamed. "Well done, my faithful servant," he said. He gently took the bowl and held it against his body.

Before the group's eyes, the bowl began to be filled with innumerable loaves of bread! The golden loaves surged into the bowl with lightning speed. "Freedom's bread," Jamal said simply.

When the bowl was filled to the brim, Jamal turned to Ursula and Lydia. "I entrust this bread to you. Go and collect your husbands. You'll find them in the grove of cherry trees where we stopped the other night. Tell them not to fear."

Without a word, Ursula took the bowl, and she and Lydia hurried away. Jamal beckoned for Brandon to approach him. Brandon saw that Jamal's eye sparkled as they stared penetratingly into his own. "You've used the Trinimal Brush, haven't you? May I see your work?"

Brandon fidgeted nervously. "It's just scribbling," he mumbled. After a moment, he shrugged and reached into his pocket.

Unrolling the parchment, he surveyed his picture before handing it to the baker. "I couldn't get the image out of my head. I worked on it all night while the others slept," he explained.

The picture shimmered with multiple colors. It depicted the execution scene. The focus of the picture was Queen Salak. She stood over Jamal's ravished body. Brandon had captured her beauty, but he'd also captured something else. Although Salak's face glowed with a crazed triumph, her eyes smouldered with a deep-rooted pain. Shadows were reflected in those ice blue eyes: shadows of unrepentance, emptiness, and, just possibly, a hint of regret.

Jamal studied the picture closely and nodded in approval. "You've captured her true identity. Well done. This picture will be our standard as we confront her. Her strength will ebb as she glimpses the truth. You will be the standard bearer."

Brandon nodded. Then the large group ran toward the battle that lay before them.

the confrontation

"Show me the prisoners!" Salak thundered. She paced before her mirror. The beautiful glass was cloudy once again. "What are you up to?" she shouted into thin air. "You're wasting your time! I've won!"

Feverishly, she continued to gaze into the looking glass. Even her own reflection was not clear! Why?

With a deafening bang, the throne room door burst open. Bovril, his face flushed crimson, ran into the room. "My Queen! Your birdcages! Your tapestries and—"

As he spoke, the ornaments on the marble-topped tables in the throne room shattered into fragments.

"Call all the soldiers!" Salak raged. Her nostrils were white with indignation, and her eyes were dilated in fear. "Search the palace for these vermin! Kill all whom you find."

As Bovril left the room, a large group of people stormed inside. At the head of the group was the familiar form of the baker! Bovril saw his queen lift her face to Jamal's. It was chalk white and wore an expression of pure terror. However, he also saw defiance smoldering within her eyes.

Salak turned her stricken face away from Jamal and surveyed the entourage of liberated prisoners. She spotted Brandon standing beside Jamal. He held aloft a picture of her. But, the picture lied! She didn't look like the grotesque monster on that parchment! Salak flinched. Quickly, she looked away, but already she felt a surge of weakness engulf her. "No!" she screamed, "You can't—"

"You are Queen of Crimilia no longer," Jamal said calmly. "Look at those you imprisoned, Salak! Even now your strength is dwindling! You can no longer feed upon their lives!"

In a flash, the queen changed into her serpent form. She lunged forward to ensnare Jamal in her scarlet coils. Instantly, Jamal's human form disappeared. He became a snow-white Lamb.

The lamb and the serpent met in a blinding flash of scarlet skin and white wool. They wrestled fiercely, Salak repeatedly attempting to sink her crimson fangs into the soft wool of Jamal's leg. Jamal's hind hoofs pinned the serpent's neck to the ground. With a mighty thrust, his front hoofs crushed the snake's head.

The serpent's body cart-whipped in a spasm of agony, and the forked tail slammed into the Mirror of Revelation.

Sparks shot into the air, and the Gems of Discord clattered to the floor.

Before the astonished eyes of the onlookers, Salak changed into a magnificent winged creature—her original Eaglia form! Her head bore a seeping wound. Even so, she glared at Jamal, who had changed back to his human form.

"I deserve to be worshiped," she said. "I am the most beautiful of all!"

Hurriedly, she tried to gather the Discord Gems, but Jamal detained her. "Only those who ask for your help will be influenced by you. You no longer have absolute power." With a lunge, his foot slammed into the cluster of gems, grinding them into a useless powder that quickly disappeared.

Jamal propelled the Eaglia toward the shattered mirror. "Look," he ordered.

Salak peered feverishly into the intact fragment of glass. The glass revealed absolutely nothing. A black hole, a void of unimaginable hugeness, was all that the crushed Eaglia could see.

"Behold who you truly are and where you are going."

Her eyes glinting, Salak turned back to Jamal. "Why?" she demanded. "Why couldn't I see them being changed? Why!"

"Because you're blind," Jamal's voice held sadness. "You blinded yourself. My Father and I lament for you." With that, the Imperial Lord's Son pushed the queen toward the mirror. The Eaglia collided with the shattered frame. Instantly, she was sucked into the empty void. The last that could be seen of her were her eyes; they shone with fear and an unrepentant defiance.

"Now, let us go," Jamal said. As the assembly left the throne room, the palace of Plenty began to shake.

Hannah stopped abruptly. She suddenly grabbed Brandon's arm. "Madeleine's in the dungeon! Come on, Brandon! You hafta help me!"

"Hannah? Are you nuts? The palace is—"

"Come on!" Pulling him forward, she broke away from the astonished group. "You hafta help me find the dungeon!"

Sighing, Brandon said, "We're gonna hafta run!"

The palace shook more and more violently. The teenagers catapulted down the multiple corridors, becoming more and more dizzy.

When they reached the dungeon, Brandon grasped Hannah's hand. "We're not going down there! If you want her, you'll hafta make her hear you."

"Madeleine! He's alive! Salak's gone! Come out!"

No sound could be heard but muffled sobs. After a moment or so, Hannah tried to speak again, but Brandon stopped her.

"You have a gift," he said. "Use it!"

Of course! Hannah began playing the longolia. Splintering wood told her that the cell door had opened. "You're worth more than you think, Madeleine," she called. "Please—"

With a crack, the dungeon stairs began to crumble. Hannah heard Madeleine scream.

"Let's go," Brandon hissed.

A hand touched Hannah's shoulder. "She has to make the decision, Hannah," Jamal's authoritative voice echoed in the collapsing building. "Your job is to deliver the message; mine is to deliver the captive. Stand aside now."

Positioning himself above the chasm that had once been dungeon steps, Jamal held out his hands. Madeleine stood for what seemed like an eternity. Then, at long last, she clasped the Deliverer's hand. Gently, he handed her a piece of Freedom's Bread and bent down.

"You must trust me. I'm going to carry you to safety."

"Why are you doing this for me?"

"Because in another world that I freed, there was a betrayer who made the wrong choice. I want everyone to taste freedom. Now we must go."

blind but now i see

When the group emerged into the sunlit day, the palace began disintegrating. "Let us go to the cherry tree grove," Jamal said.

The black fog had lifted, and the Tapestry of Safety had vanished. In its place was another tapestry: a picture of a life-size baker's oven that shone with a wondrous radiance. Brilliant sunlight and a gentle breeze fell upon the group of followers as they stood in the grove of cherry trees. The Memorium Tree shimmered in the distance– an emblem that would never disappear. Along with the liberated prisoners, Marshall, Mendel, Samenal, Barson, Angela, Jumria, and her little girl gathered around the baker.

"All of you have done well," Jamal said. "I must leave you now, for I have other countries to protect, but I will return in time and take you to a prepared place so that you may live with me forever. You will not be alone. The Comfort-Giver and Guide, the Pure Alurian, is coming. He will assist you.

"Now, I appoint a king and queen to rule." He pointed to Samenal and Lydia.

Samenal's face crumpled. "You trust me, my Lord? But I deserted you. I've committed murder."

Jamal nodded. "A new day has dawned. I instruct all of you to go throughout Crimilia. Offer Freedom's Bread to every person whom you encounter. Those who accept the bread accept me, for I am the bread."

He turned to Ursula, who held the overflowing bowl of loaves. "This bowl will never be empty, and the bread will never grow stale," he said.

Then Jamal gestured to Hannah and Brandon. "Please come with me," he said.

The two teenagers followed the Deliverer of Crimilia farther into the grove of trees. Brandon recognized the spot as the place where Jamal had prayed a few nights earlier.

"Both of you did excellent work," he said. "Are you now ready to return to your world?"

Hannah's face fell. "I feel at home here now. Will we ever see you again?"

Jamal's eyes twinkled. "You can count on it. But don't look for me in Crimilia. Look for me in your own world. I think you'll find that I'm always close by, even if my name is different."

"Do you remember when you asked me if I believed you could restore my sight?" Hannah asked.

Jamal nodded.

"I do believe," Hannah said. "But I don't want you to. I can see something much better now."

Brandon was nodding in agreement with Hannah's words.

Jamal enfolded both of them into his arms. He said nothing, but there was no need.

"Will everyone here be all right?" Brandon asked. "Is Salak really gone for good?"

Jamal frowned slightly. "Her physical form is gone from Crimilia," he said, "but her influence still remains. As I told her, she is available only to those who ask her for help. Be on your guard. Although she may not appear in the form you met in Crimilia, she is already in your world. Her spirit travels from world to world, seeking to devour them all."

Hannah nodded in understanding.

"Now I will send you home," Jamal said. "Thank you both for your help."

He reached out a hand and gave Hannah a wooden object. Hannah's hands explored it. "A cane!" she cried. Relief flowed through her. Now she didn't feel lost! "Thanks!"

Jamal's eyes twinkled. "I haven't forgotten you, Brandon." He handed Brandon a wooden crutch.

Brandon stared at the tool. "Thanks, but I can walk without—"

Jamal looked at him with piercing eyes. "Your noble action on the bus caused you pain," he said.

Brandon suddenly remembered the deer that had smashed into the bus. He remembered the blinding pain in his bad leg.

"Thanks," he repeated. Then, he turned to Hannah. "When we get home, do you wanna maybe go to the movies or something?"

Hannah grinned. "Sure," she said.

Jamal raised his hands and touched Hannah and Brandon's shoulders. The world tilted, and blackness engulfed them.

was it a dream?

"Hannah? Hannah? You cried out. Are you all right?" A familiar voice pierced Hannah's eardrums.

Dazed, Hannah tried to sit up. "No, hon. Lie still now."

Hannah nodded. Her head ached. "Ms. Maplewood?" she croaked.

"That's right. You're in Mercy Hospital. You have a mild concussion, but you'll be fine. You're mom will be here in a minute."

"The bus—" Hannah began. "The other kids! Mr. Peterson! Brandon—"

"Calm down now. Everyone's all right. Brand's leg's broken, but he'll be fine. The bus is totaled, of course."

"I'm sorry I've been such a jerk," Hannah blurted.

"Hey. You've gone through something no one should have to endure," Ms. Maplewood said. A surprised note was in her voice. "Just lie down now and get some sleep."

"When Mom comes in, I'm going to talk to her about taking music lessons again," Hannah said. She couldn't seem to stop the flow of words that gushed from her. It was as if a fountain in her soul had been released.

"It'll be nice to hear music in the house again," Ms. Maplewood said. "Since you seem to be in good spirits, do you want anything now?"

"A Coke would be good."

"Sure. I'll be right back."

The housekeeper headed for the door. Before she reached it, she turned back. "Your cane is by the bed. It looks different, somehow, and when they brought you to the hospital, you had something clutched in your hand. They could barely pry it from your fingers! It looked like some sort of instrument. It's on the table beside you."

The door closed softly behind the retreating form.

Hannah's heart began to pound. It wasn't a dream!

"Thanks, Jamal," she whispered. Then she retrieved her longolia and began to play.

listen|imagine|view|experience

AUDIO BOOK DOWNLOAD INCLUDED WITH THIS BOOK!

In your hands you hold a complete digital entertainment package. In addition to the paper version, you receive a free download of the audio version of this book. Simply use the code listed below when visiting our website. Once downloaded to your computer, you can listen to the book through your computer's speakers, burn it to an audio CD or save the file to your portable music device (such as Apple's popular iPod) and listen on the go!

How to get your free audio book digital download:

1. Visit www.tatepublishing.com and click on the e|LIVE logo on the home page.
2. Enter the following coupon code: 1ef7-c489-ee19-46a9-8c84-104a-c809-2c4c
3. Download the audio book from your e|LIVE digital locker and begin enjoying your new digital entertainment package today!